THOMAS R CLARK

<u>ALSO BY THE AUTHOR</u>

GOOD BOY
BELLA'S BOYS
THE DEATH LIST
THE GOD PROVIDES
A PRAYER FROM THE DEAD
IMMORAL DILEMMAS
WE ARE 13

<u>COMING SOON</u>

WHIRLWIND
THE CURSE OF KATIE ELDER
THE WITCH OF NOVEMBER
THE TELLING OF THE BEES

A DESPERATE PLAN

Ronnie Dark sat at the kitchen table, a notepad before him, chewing on a ballpoint pen cap. He stared at the paper, afraid to write the words. He started to second guess his motivations. He lost his job, his wife, his luggage, and his house. Luggage was luggage; it would come back to him at some point. He could get another woman; those were easy. Without a place to live, getting a new job would be even more difficult. He felt the anger coming back. His hand shook as the pen greeted the paper.

Dear Bitch, *he wrote, then stopped. He ripped the paper off the pad, crumpled it, and tossed it into a nearby trash bin. It joined a dozen other attempts he'd made in the past hour. Why was it so hard to write a suicide note? Robert E. Howard did it easily enough prior to blowing his brains out with a .380 Colt eighty years before.*

"All Fled, all done, so lift me on the pyre, the feast is over and the lamps expired." The writer left the paraphrased lines from Viola Garvin's The Fall of Caesar in his typewriter. Then bang! All because his mother died.

The manner in which he would end his own life was yet to be determined. The ways to take your own life were prolific. So, in lieu of writing his suicide note, Ronnie first compiled a list from which he could narrow down his choice of euthanasia. He wrote Death List *across the top of the paper in big bold letters, followed by his options...*

THOMAS R CLARK

THE DEATH LIST: REMASTERED

THIRD EDITION
ISBN: 979-8-9991091-4-9
THE DEATH LIST © 2019
THE DEATH LIST © DECEMBER 2023
THE DEATH LIST: REMASTERD © JULY 2025
Published by Stitched Smile Publications
© 2020 By Thomas R Clark
All Rights Reserved.
Cover design by Thomas R. Clark
© 2020 by Thomas R Clark
Interior Plate Designs by Thomas R Clark
and Deborah Coldiron

THOMAS R CLARK

THE DEATH LIST

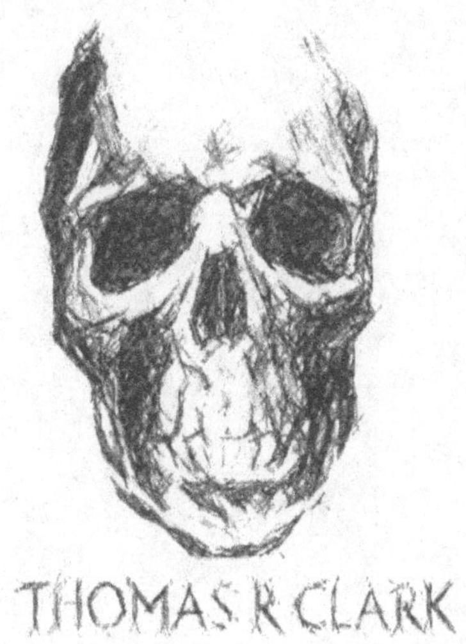

STITCHED SMILE PUBLICATIONS
HOUSTON, TX

CHAPTER 1

RONNIE & THE LETTER

FRIDAY, JUNE 11, 2021 10:00 P.M.

Dear Melissa,

Surprise, bitch!!! Do you like what I left for you? Considering the circumstances, I thought it was the most appropriate gift I've ever given someone, even an ungrateful, cunting whore like you.

I want you to smell my rotted corpse forever. I want you to see it in your dreams, burned into your retinas. I want you to see it everywhere. when you walk into the fucking living room, when you get up in the night to take a piss, when you open your fucking Christmas gifts with fat boy. I want to fuck your mouth with the sweet, sick putrid aroma of my bloated corpse, tasting my decaying flesh on your tongue until you gag.

I want to be your undead hag in the bathtub

from room 237 at the Overlook Hotel, busting down the door with an ax, screaming "Here's Ronnie!" I want you to remember my dead body every time Clarence sticks his little cock in your ass, because that's the only way you'll feel it. Lord knows that canyon you call a cunt won't. I want you to think of the blowflies circling around my body, and how long it took you to get them out of the house as he grunts like a little pig.

You're probably wondering why? Why did Ronnie do this? First of all, since I took my own life and made a spectacle of it, there isn't any life insurance for you. But this little tidbit is just the tip of my dead dick fucking you from the afterlife.

You, my dear Melissa, are a skanky, used-up whore and you stomped on my heart.

I fucking hate you!

You ruined me and took everything I ever earned, and for these crimes against my humanity, you will pay. This is my final gift to you, the gift that keeps giving. I'm going to be immortal. I'm going to live for eternity in every waking moment. I'm going to show up when you least expect it, or need me to. I'm going to

haunt you until the day you fucking die.
  I loved you,
  Ronnie

•

Ronnie Dark slammed the pen on the table and stepped away. Paul Revere and the Raiders warned him about kicks, the soundtrack airing from smart speakers set about the house. It was time to go to the shed and get the tools needed to get the job done. For the first time in a week, Ronnie smiled. The song changed, replaced by the perfect piece. "B.F.D.R.F.B." Big fucking deal. Rat fink blues. Not even the Beatles grew the balls to record something like it. And it's why Paul Revere and the Raiders were the coolest thing to come out of the Sixties.

He gazed out the windows overlooking the property as the song played, losing himself in the melody. The darkness turned the panes of glass into translucent mirrors. The reflection of the clock in the kitchen was a ghost image on the glass. It gave the illusion of time ticking off, counting backwards. Hypnotic, it carried

Ron's memories from their home, deep in the recesses of his mind, back into the present...

CHAPTER 2

PATRICK &
JOHN-JOHN

SATURDAY, OCTOBER 13, 1984, 11:50 P.M.

John-John Dermotty was pissed. When he got home, he was gonna jack somebody's ass. His little brother's, more than likely. He doubted Mom or Dad found the roofies in his jean jacket pocket, which left one culprit: Patrick. It was the little shit's fault John-John didn't get laid tonight. The bastard would pay for it, in spades. The long drive home from Kingston to their "mansion" in the mountains gave him plenty of time to think about it.

There was no easy way to get there. His father felt it was best for the kids if they moved to the suburbs from the Big Apple. John-John discovered the hard way Dad's idea of suburbs was in the middle of the woods. The house was isolated, located on a dead-end private road off Route 28A. Any road leading to the remote property went around the Ashokan Reservoir, making travel to and from the house a tedious affair.

This put a serious dampening on John-John's fucking. The Catskills were full of those freaky looking Hasidic Jews with their black clothes and curls, hiding behind chain-link fences and concertina wire. He passed by one of the compounds they lived in. The dormitories reminded him of a detention center. It wasn't a fertile proving ground for a virulent young man such as he.

After all, John-John was the eldest of the Dermotty's two children by seven years. And he was junior to real estate mogul Jack Dermotty Senior. But none of these accolades mattered when you lived on the edge of civilization. The closest major city was Kingston, over a half hour's drive away because of the curving country roads. The isolation was his own personal chastity prison.

Tonight was a wasted trip to the mall in Kingston. He realized too late the pills weren't in the pocket of his jean jacket. Prissy Peggy Wells was his date, and she was notorious for not putting out. John-John set out to conquer Peggy's virtue, with a little pharmaceutical assistance, but it wasn't happening. He couldn't so much as cop a feel on one of her budding titties. John-John, a lifelong New York Yankees fan, could relate to the Bronx Bombers of late, always stranding guys on first base. All thanks to Patrick.

John-John thought he might start by taking Patrick's wrestling action figures. Melting them before him might trigger some response. The little bastard was always carrying one of them around with him. Then he'd magnetize the video cassettes of the Gladiator movies the kid couldn't stop watching. He shook with anticipation as he neared their home, driving a new Chrysler K-Car his father swore by. John-John didn't have the heart to tell his dad the car was a piece of shit. The back seat was a bitch to fuck in too.

John-John pulled into the driveway of their house and parked the car. He hopped out and closed the door, not bothering to lock it. After all, who would be bothered with hiking over a mountain to break into their cars? Let alone a piece of crap K-Car?

Something was off.

The bugs, he thought as the eerie silence

took hold. *Where are their chirps and buzzes?* The forest was alive at night, but not this night. *Is it the weather?* John-John wondered. He walked in through the garage's open bay door. Except for the muffled sound of a television on somewhere in the house, John-John found his home to be dark and quiet. This was odd. Wasn't Patrick having a sleepover with his friends? *Damn*, he thought, *these kids are well behaved*. Soon as they left in the morning, Patrick would pay for his sins.

Snacks and a cooler of some mystery drink sat on the kitchen table. John-John helped himself to a plastic cup full of what turned out to be iced cold lime Kool-Aid, his favorite. He drank it down, sighed in relief, crumpled the plastic cup, and dropped it into a waste can.

He crept upstairs, being careful to not make any noise. He wasn't about waking up any of the visitors, or his parents for the matter. John-John was also late coming home, and though his father was a pushover, his mother Shirley was a raging bitch when he got out of line. Now he was a senior in high school, and he'd graduated from the wooden or metal slotted spoons across his ass to full-on face smacking. She could be ruthless.

The upstairs bathroom light was still on, which caught his attention. His mother was a stickler for the lights being shut off when you weren't in a room. He tiptoed down the hall, ever so silent. When he was within an arm's length of the shitter, he reached in with one hand, felt about, flicked off the light switch, and made his way back toward his bedroom.

John-John's path led past his parents' bedroom, exposing him to another chance of discovery by his militant mother. Anxiety caused him to shake. He felt the bottom of his belly fall out, a pit of despair growing within. He saw in the dim light their bedroom door was open, another anomaly he didn't expect.

Fuck! He cursed himself. Mom was notorious for being a light sleeper. He crept on by, ducking and making his profile as small as he could, hopping past his parents' bedroom on the balls of his feet. Acid reflux burned his throat; he tasted bile. A tense minute passed and he was safe, within the confines of his own bedroom. Not bothering to turn the lights on, John-John disrobed and slid under both the sheet and comforter.

Visions of inflicting pain and suffering upon Patrick's being danced in his head as John-John made a vain attempt to fall asleep. After ten minutes of climbing into bed, the sour feeling in his stomach got worse. The room was spinning. He dropped a foot over the side of the mattress to try and stop it, but the attempt made him more nauseous.

John-John jumped out of the bed, throwing the covers aside, and ran into the hallway. He no longer cared if he woke Mom up. She'd be more pissed if he puked on the floor. He felt drunk, like he did after binge drinking, shot-gunning Genny Screamers. It was well over a week since any alcohol touched his lips. John-John felt the contents of his stomach rising, but they wouldn't come out. He held back, his diaphragm convulsing, desperately wanting to dry heave at the least. His eyes were clenched shut and he held his breath; he feared letting either go would result in an acidic purge on the carpets. His mother would destroy him. He threw himself into the bathroom, flipped the light switch, fell to his knees at the toilet bowl, and dropped his head.

His face slapped into something cold and

wet. He smelled something rancid. His lips, pursed as they were, allowed some of it to sneak through to the tip of his tongue. It was coppery with hints of sulfur. He jerked back from the toilet seat and opened his eyes.

Shirley Dermotty sat on the toilet before him, lifeless eyes staring back at her son. She was covered in blood, wearing something resembling a crown on her head. At first, John-John wasn't sure what it was made of, but it looked like a heart made of sausage links. Each one was about eight inches long, spilling from his mother's abdomen, which was flayed open in a single long cut. Somebody made a wreath out of her intestines and placed it on her head.

John-John opened his lips to scream. Instead of a wail, vomit, ripe with bile and popcorn kernels from his movie earlier in the night, exploded from his mouth. It splattered across his mother's bloody corpse, causing her to list to one side. Her head tipped with her body, but the intestinal crown remained affixed. The guts squeaked across the porcelain tiles covering the wall.

Her teenage son slipped on the gore

covered linoleum flooring, moving as fast as he could. He fell forward out of the bathroom. John-John crawled on his hands and knees down the hallway. His palms and legs left bloody orange prints and streaks on the yellow carpeting behind him. Vertigo prevented him from standing. Lucky for him, it seemed the floor moved in unison. Mostly. He bounced off the wall with his shoulder, using it to maintain his forward momentum.

He burst into his parents' bedroom, tumbling on the floor. Looking up, he didn't need to turn the lights on to know his father, too, was dead. Diffused light, enhanced by the large flood lamp illuminating the yard outside their window, outlined the family patriarch. John Dermotty, Sr. looked tarred, awaiting the feathers. John-John father's teeth glistened in the dim light, further adding to the stereotype unfolding before the teenager. The elder Dermotty called his perfect white chompers the Million Dollar Smile, and credited them, more than anything else, for his success as a car salesman. Jack was sitting up in bed, not moving, holding an animal of some sort in his arms. John-John could discern the ears, snout, and tubular tail bookending the creature. It might have been a small dog or a large rabbit.

Except the Dermottys owned no pets.

John-John grasped the door frame, pulling himself to a vertical base. The room spun as he rose, almost causing him to fall. He took a moment to catch his balance. His mother and father both were disemboweled, their intestines tied off into gruesome sculptures.

What is going on here? What about the ...

Kids!

John-John, still unsure of his ability to stand, let alone move, launched down the hall to the stairs. He skipped three, then four steps, before crashing onto the landing and twisting, falling down the final three steps to the floor. Vertigo and gravity won. He landed in a clump, jamming both hands into the wall. One broke through the painted drywall, the other made a good dent. His head banged off it next, striking in the middle between his hands. The stunned teenager saw a shape move toward him from the family room and where he assumed the kids were sleeping.

He recognized his brother's WWF T-shirt

through the blood covering it. The red of the shirt was darker than it should have been, but John-John could make out the caricature of the champion flexing his twenty-four-inch pythons. Covering his brother's face was a pro-wrestler's mask, one from Dad's private collection.

John-John recognized the mask as being one his father prized. Black with red eye slits, it resembled a dragon's face. Jack Dermotty was a lifelong wrestling fan, and Patrick ate it up. He often invited pro-wrestlers to make public appearances at the dealership, something little Patrick loved. It was now evident his brother's enthusiasm went a few steps too far.

Something shiny glared in his brother's hand; it was difficult to focus on. John-John realized too late the item was a short Gladiator sword. Time slowed; he tried processing where his brother would have found the sword. The blade was black and short, but longer than Patrick's leg. The boy dragged the sword behind him; it scraped across the carpeting, the tip cutting a slit in the fabric.

Patrick swung the heavy sword like a

baseball bat in slow motion.

John-John admired the craftsmanship of the sword's handle as it rocketed toward him. Strips of black leather crisscrossed the grip from pommel to guard creating a pattern of diamonds exposing miscellaneous precious gems in varying hues of red.

The sword pommel connected with his temple. It was temporary relief, jarring everything back to normal for a moment. Time snapped back to normal with each passing moment before unconsciousness set in. It gave John Dermotty, Jr. one last moment of clarity, and an epiphany, if you will. He realized why he felt drunk and where the roofies he planned to drug Prissy Peggy with went.

The fucking Kool-Aid. He roofied the fucking Kool-Aid and I drank it!

Everything went black for a second, or so he thought. He squinted at stars and a dull roar of thunder. Then John-John shook his head and woke up in a haze. No longer feeling drunk, he knew something was off with his body. He felt weak; something as simple as moving his head took a monumental effort.

He was out long enough for somebody to

move him. He saw he was in their family room. A Steve Reeves Hercules Sword and Sandals flick played on the VCR. It was a grainy picture, recorded off HBO, with streaks and lines from overuse decorating the picture on the family's big-screen TV.

He was cold and naked, laying in a large puddle of black and sticky blood covering the floor. All around John-John were the boys from Patrick's school. Each one was lined up next to the other, nice and neat in a row, all naked and with their stomachs cut open. Patrick had molded their large intestines into unique shapes, displayed with pride on the individual bodies. A dog here, a cat there, a beetle, a fire engine. All in total a half dozen sculptures crafted from the eviscerated guts of Patrick's classmates. He assumed they were all dead, as he wasn't in any condition to go about checking for pulses. However, judging from their exsanguinated appearances, staring at the ceiling with cold, white eyes, he was pretty sure his assumption was accurate.

"Patrick, what is going on?" John-John tried to say, but the words came out as a whisper. He didn't have the strength to project them. Each word took a monumental effort to even think of, let alone to put into a sentence.

"John-John Dermotty! Come on down! You're the next sacrifice to Saint D'Inana!" He heard his brother's voice come from under the mask, mimicking the game show hosts he adored. "She wanted me to make gifts for everyone tonight, gifts for the children to take with them, gifts for the adults to take with them, everyone here in the studio audience! I even made you a gift, big brother!"

"What kind of gifts, Patrick?" John-John was terrified of the answer his brother would give.

"Why gifts made with your help, of course!"

John-John saw his brother holding a turtle, except it wasn't. It was red and slimy, with black spots. The shell wasn't solid, it was contoured, a series of fingers laid side by side. As Patrick lifted it forward, John-John felt a tug at his midsection. He sucked in as much air as he could muster the strength to do. Stinging pain wracked his back and ribs and abdomen as he did so. His fingers and toes felt cold, his nose too.

"What have you done, Patrick? What have

you done?"

"Well, considering you gave an answer in the form of a question, the judges have approved your request for an explanation of the rules of the game." Patrick's voice turned into a little boy's tone and timber, one John-John was familiar with. It somehow gave the words he said a bigger impact. "Saint D'Inana told me you deserved the turtle because of what you do to the girls. I didn't want to believe her, but she showed me what was in your dresser drawer, where you keep the panties of the girls you did bad things to. And the pills in your pocket. Shame on you, big brother! It's okay, though, Saint D'Inana told me once you have your gift, you will be free."

John-John heard his brother's gleeful voice resonate in his head, not unlike any other ten-year-old boy excited about a new toy. The chill in his extremities was traveling throughout his body now. How Patrick knew about his stash of trophies and what he did with the pills was perplexing him. Who was this Saint D'Inana he kept mentioning? What was he talking about?

"So here's your gift, John-John. I'll see you

on the other side when Saint D'Inana tells me it's time for me to join you with them."

"Them?" Blood drooled down John-John's chin as he asked the question.

"All the sacrifices, silly! I've got so much to do until then. Right now, I have to put Saint D'Inana back in her box under the shed. They're going to take me away for a little while, big brother." Patrick handed his brother the turtle. John-John was given no choice but to accept it. His hands collapsed onto his lap, still clutching the balloon animal crafted from his own large and small intestines. "Until next time," the game show host voice returned, "this is Patrick Dermotty saying, 'Don't forget to filet and neuter your guests!'"

Patrick walked away, dragging the black sword behind him. He was humming the theme to *The Price is Right*. The melody drifted into a fog John-John couldn't break away from. The tune fell further and more distant with each shallow breath John-John could manage to make. With his diaphragm sliced through, it was difficult. Finally, there was silence, and John Dermotty Jr. heard nothing at all, ever again.

CHAPTER 3

RONNIE & THE PLAN

FRIDAY, JUNE 11, 2021, 6:00 P.M.

*W*hat *is worse?* Ronnie Dark mused. *A divorce, losing your job, or the airport losing your luggage?* He decided the answer was D, all of the above. *Plus you're homeless for the double bonus win!*

Earlier in the day, he stood on the porch of his house …

House? Call it what it is! A mansion in the Catskill Mountains of New York.

… holding a legal document in his hand. The papers, once taped to his door, were printed in all caps. Ron stared in disbelief at the words as he read the legalese. They blindsided him, stealing his breath and stopping his heart for a beat, or three.

"Ronald Richard Dick, Jr. (Respondent) is hereby ordered to remove himself from the premises within forty-eight (48) hours of receipt of this legal deposition."

He was given two days to vacate the

premises, otherwise known as his home of over a quarter-century. All because of his wife of as many years.

Well, ex-wife now, he supposed.

She delivered the final blow to his ego and already fragile psyche during their ugly break up over the past week. Melissa Dick, aka Melissa Dark, set her husband up for a fall. He bought it all the way down.

"Fuck you, you fucking twatwaffle, cunting whore! The fucking fuck, fuck, fuck!" He kicked the cedar shingle siding of the porch. It deflected his blow, sending him on his ass. He landed in a clump with the eviction notice grasped in his outstretched fist while continuing to shout every conceivable variant of fuck and cunt he could manage. He slammed his forearms onto the deck.

Ronnie took a moment to regain his composure. He stood up, straightened his clothing, and smoothed out the wrinkled eviction notice. He flipped open the security panel and entered the code, carefully pressing 7-1-6-9 on the keypad.

"Sixty-nine with two fingers in the ass, bitch!" He declared as he punched in the numbers, hitting the nine with his middle and index fingers. His fingertips stung from the impact, and he felt a tender spot growing on the forefinger. The alarm chirped, releasing the electric locks on the door.

He entered his home for the next two days, slamming the door behind him. The house was dark. He didn't bother turning on any lights; the ambient sunlight entering through the windows was enough to see by. The foyer's tall, thirty-two-foot cathedral ceiling cast shadows into the dining room and the kitchen set off to the side. Semi-transparent shades were drawn on a series of six bay windows along the building's front. Anyone sitting in the living room would have a view of the rolling forest surrounding the mansion.

Ronnie dropped the papers in his hand on an end table and walked with determination to the liquor cabinet. Behind it, Ron found the bottle of Jack Daniels he got from Beaver last Christmas.

"Alexa, play Paul Revere and the Raiders for me!" The home's smart sound system played "Cherokee Nation". Ronnie loved The Raiders. The pop sensibility of the songs, the theatrics of it all. It gave him a brief moment of repose from his helpless situation. "Fuck-ah you-ah, mange," he said, unscrewing the cap off the whiskey and pouring a rock glass full of bourbon, "and fuck my fucking whore wife!" He downed the contents. Setting it back on the bar with a clink, he refilled it and drained it again without hesitation. "Son of a fucking bitch!" The repetitive pattern of filling and draining the rock glass, interspersed with varying forms of fuck as a verb, adjective, and/or noun, continued until the bottle was empty.

Ron collapsed on a nearby leather sofa, spreading out across its length. Lost in his thoughts, tinnitus ringing in his ears, he wept. His sniffing sounded shallow in the expanse of the 30,000-square-foot mansion. Other than the sound created by its sole occupant, the building was silent with no ambient noise. It reminded Ron of a tomb, a vast mausoleum housing dead memories, the sofa an open casket.

Thoughts raced through his brain. What would he do? Where would he go? Motherfucker! What the fuck did I do to deserve this ass fucking? Ron sat up and screamed, his voice bouncing off the cold, dark walls. No one answered. He hung his head between his hands, elbows pressed into his thighs just above the knee. And then it came to him. When he left this place, he wouldn't have jack shit. It wasn't a material object issue; the fact was Ron would be homeless.

"Just Like Me", another of his Raiders favorites, came to life. It made Ronnie feel more isolated. He was left with nothing to live for. No job. No money. No fans. There was nobody there for him. No children. No real friends. He might have one friend of a sort: the Dark's former lead singer Steve Brodie, lived in Kingston, but they talked on rare occasions. His father, Ron Dick, Sr., Ronnie's last living blood relative, passed away a decade before. He was destitute. Until today, his only possessions were this house and its contents. And it was all gone, taken by a rotten bitch who lied and told him she'd be with him for better or worse. Melissa, the love of his life, she took it all from him, including his dignity.

He was always a generous partner, or at

least he believed he was. Ron bought his wife a bouquet of flowers every Friday for over thirty years. After letting them brighten the house for a day or two, she donated the arrangements to local funerals before they became less than presentable. Anything she wanted, Ron gave Melissa. Yeah, he conceded, maybe his career choice took him away from the house a little more than she would like. His latest gig of playing in cover bands on cruise ships took him away for weeks at a time. He couldn't help this aspect of his line of work; it came with the job description of cruise ship musician. He felt lucky not catching Covid the year before. But not working for a year took its toll on what little money he put away. Besides, she knew what she was getting into when she married a rock star. One day the star would fade.

What did she give him in return? Nothing. She took everything. These thoughts raced through his brain. He started writing a song in his head. It's what he did when drunk and lamenting. The writing was cathartic for him in the past and helped him heal any emotional baggage troubling him. But now, it was a grim reminder. Nothing was all there was left to give her. But no, that wasn't right. There was something.

"I got nothing left to give you," he sang, "except myself."

"Fuck this. Fuck ever buying this cursed fucking place. I've had nothing but bad luck since I bought a god-motherfucking-damn murder house!"

The bourbon thinned his blood to the point where gravity made moving from the sofa an OSHA violation. Ronnie remembered the signs in the employee lounges on the cruise line, thumbtacked to a corkboard declaring *Number of Days Without An Accident* followed by a variable integer. He pissed himself where he sat. The numerals on the imaginary sign in his head flipped backwards to zero. The urine pooled on the leather, then dripped onto the floor in a steady pattern, ticking the minutes away. Listening to the steady drip, drip, drip,.. Ronnie found a moment of clarity and knew the answer. A special housewarming gift was in order. A gift she'd never forget.

Ron would leave her a conversation piece. Visitors to her home would whisper and gossip about the sordid details, giving them an excuse not to attend functions. A self-propagating gift, the kind to keep giving until she followed him to her grave. He would give her all there was left to give. The one thing she would never expect or ever want. Something so appropriate for the location, another mystery adding to the legend of an infamous murder house.

His own dead and stinking body.

CHAPTER 4

PATRICK & KATIE

WEDNESDAY, JUNE 9, 2021, 11:09 P.M.

If Katie White were alive, she would have heard the live news report on the big TV in her bedroom. Instead, she lay upon her bed, dead and nude, her upper body and hair slick with blood. Her knees were bent and apart.

Inmate on the loose scrolled across the red and white marquee on the screen, indicating breaking news.

"The suspect, Patrick Dermotty, also known as the Balloon Boy Killer, should be considered extremely dangerous," a middle-aged man told the viewing audience. "Any civilians encountering this person should remain at a safe distance and contact authorities. County-wide manhunts in Onondaga, Oswego, and Cayuga counties are in effect. Police have set up roadblocks on all roads in a twenty-mile radius surrounding the city of Fenton."

Something wet and red was splashed across the screen, obscuring the video footage of the Fenton State Hospital grounds. Hanging outside of Katie's vagina was a fleshy mess. Pink tubes and entrails were dripping off the edge of the bed and draping onto the floor. If the television reporter interviewed her corpse, she would have told him it was her lovely Patrick. He'd done this to her.

Hours before, alone in her used Lexus, Katie White smoked a joint while scrolling through social media on her telephone. Her break time was her time, and she wouldn't spend it in the hospital's break room with the staff. They annoyed her. They didn't understand or get Katie; she knew it, so she excluded herself from them during social gatherings. Interactions with her co-workers were polite but brief and direct with no small talk.

She was there for the patients, not the personnel. The poor, lost souls were her charge. She swore an oath to aid the sick and needy, so tend to them, she would. Especially the broken minds in Fenton State Hospital for the Criminally Insane.

One patient in particular gained her trust and attention during the last decade she'd spent tending to him. Patrick Dermotty, aka The Balloon Boy. Pat never spoke, not once. In the ten years Katie worked at Fenton, he sat in his dorm room, a stoic, silent sentinel guarding the secrets to why he massacred a house full of people thirty-five years ago. He fascinated her to the point he became an obsession. The media portrayed Patrick as an insane murderer. Katie knew this wasn't the case. He was misunderstood, not in control of his faculties when the murders were committed. Plus it was over thirty years ago; he was a different person now. All he did was sit in his room watching game shows. He never spoke, not once. He was as much an innocent victim now as the people he murdered thirty years before.

She opened her glove compartment. She pulled a bit of folded black cloth out from inside, then closed it, the lock popping into place. She unfolded the cloth. It was a wrestler's mask, black with a horrifying white dragon's face stitched into the material. She grasped it in her hand, feeling the fabric on her skin. It was exhilarating.

A condom advertisement appeared on the screen of her phone. Katie chuckled at the thought. Why would her ad bots play this spot? Who would she have sex with? She'd been single since college, and celibate by choice, waiting for the hand of the right guy to come along.

The joint burned out as its THC coursed through her body, releasing serotonin and dopamine into her being. Katie still held the mask in her hand, but it fell to her lap, laying across her crotch. She pressed it down; a finger rubbed the indentation of her vulva through her cotton scrubs and the mask's nylon.

Who would I want to have sex with? She thought as her vagina moistened in excitement.

There was only one man.

Later in the night, she would take Patrick Dermotty out for a, well, let's call it what it was: furlough for a conjugal visit. Prescribed by Nurse White, of course. Patrick, silent and solemn as always, didn't complain when she escorted him out of the ward, sneaking him past security and into her Lexus. No one asked her any questions. Why would they?

She drove him straight to her house. She lived about twenty miles from Fenton, in another dying upstate New York city, Fulton. In a one-two punch twenty-five years earlier, Fulton lost its aluminum can plant. Not long after, the good graces of chocolatiers Nestle followed suit. The economically depressed city still hadn't recovered and was fast becoming a graveyard of empty factories. In a few short minutes, she presumed, her house would become another standing casket in the cemetery known as Fulton, New York.

Once home, she planned to consummate their relationship with due haste. Patrick, too, wished to proceed with the pleasantries. His idea of how to please a woman, though, wasn't conventional, Katie soon learned. The foreplay started out innocent enough. She stripped down and spread her legs wide open for him.

"Touch me," Katie told Patrick. He did. She felt his soft hand, each finger on his ham-fist a sex toy in its own right. She wanted to feel all of him inside her. She grabbed his hand

and forced her vagina down on it. She felt herself stretch to accommodate the size of his appendage. First his fingers, then they slipped past the first knuckle. Katie felt as if he was splitting her in half but didn't care. She was losing her virginity all over again, to the man she'd loved the past ten years.

She felt his fingers around her cervix plunging deeper into her vagina, stimulating the nerves in the back wall, nerves she'd never felt such pleasure from before. She felt his hand move back and forth, fucking her. Ecstasy flooded her body with hormones. Her eyes fluttered as orgasm after orgasm released dopamine into her system. He went deeper and harder with each thrust.

Then he stopped, and she felt a finger tracing the edges of her rectum. It felt so good. So sinful. She pushed her ass onto his finger.

And a second one entered her anus.

Then a third.

She pushed and squirmed on his hand, and it sank deeper into her rectum. The ring of muscle relaxed, opening wider. He thrust three, then four fingers, in and out, up to the knuckle, in time with his other hand, still buried in her vagina. She clenched her rectum around his wrist and felt waves of pleasure as he stimulated the nerve endings.

Then she felt a strange sensation inside her, all through her. She looked down and saw his arm was thrust into her ass up to the elbow.

Incredible cramps shot fiery irons of pain through her belly and diaphragm. She felt something tickling her abdomen and looked at it. Fingers were poking up, stretching the flesh like Playdough. Katie heard a ripping sound as Patrick removed his hand from her prolapsing asshole, bringing with it a handful of pink and black entrails.

He crafted her a gift; how could he not? Before he left, he spoke to her for the first, and only time, in the decade they'd been acquainted. She'd never forget the words, she told herself. They were sweet and articulate.

"This is Patrick Dermotty, saying bye-bye, and I hope you got the date you really wanted." His words were calm and deliberate, if not a bit extravagant in their pronunciation. Almost like a gameshow host saying goodbye, she mused. He'd given her the date she always wanted, and more. He kissed her forehead, then donned the wrestling mask she'd procured for him. He stretched it over his head and tied the laces behind his neck.

She smiled, having been satisfied for the first time in her now shortened life, and closed her eyes. It was okay. Her last breath exhaled as the news report broke for commercial. The last thing Katie would ever hear wasn't Patrick's voice. It was a car salesman and a former Syracuse University lineman telling her and some guy named Tom to go to Adams, New York, for something *Huge!*

•

An hour later, the same door was smashed in and a Special Ops squad moved through the home with tactical precision. Displayed on the bed was Kathleen Elizabeth White's mutilated body and Patrick Dermotty's gift to her. A heart, crafted from her fallopian tubes, with a neat bow tie made of small intestine, sat on the mattress next to her corpse.

When the all clear was given, a woman of

importance and her personal bodyguards entered the premises. To her left stood a dark skinned woman with piercing blue eyes. To her right, a tall, thin white man, his face partially covered by mirrored sunglasses and riddled by acne scarring. One of the special ops team addressed her, a pair of parallel bars in black powder coat pinned to his lapel.

"He's gone, Doctor Pennoire."

"I can see that, Captain. How far can he get on foot? Or car from here? This is fucking Fulton, the West Virginia of Upstate, New York. I haven't seen this many Confederate flags this far north in my life. For fuck's sake! How far could he get?"

"We'll find him, Doctor."

"You're damn right you'll find him. If you don't, there's going to be a body count we don't want to explain to the press. Somebody get me the phone numbers of anyone else who might have touched this guy's file in the past thirty years. Time to let the State boys in on our little secret." The special ops captain turned and rallied the bodyguards.

Pennoire stayed behind, losing herself in thought. The doctor was pissed. She should have seen this in White's personality profile. But she didn't. She thought back, then cursed herself for not seeing the pattern.

For a decade, a woman skilled at hiding her bi-polar phases from her employers was entrusted with the care of the most violent offenders in the State hospital. The frightful four that many of the other nurses feared, but not Kathleen White. It was now obvious she felt something other than fear for them; a sinful feeling, one she could never tell anyone. She could have blamed her obsession on daddy issues, but it was more a kindred feeling she shared. Dubbed the Middle Ages Dungeon, because each of them was now in their 40s and 50s, three of them lived in the facility since their youths, the fourth came in as an adult. And Nurse White lived in a prison all her life too. Her experience was much more intimate, hands on with patients ... as opposed to having racked up a massive triple digit kill total in the outside world.

First, the eldest of the bunch, Lewis Lent was also the least worrisome of the lot. He'd only kidnapped one girl in the 90s: Ms. Sara Wood, a pastor's daughter. A wild goose chase with authorities led to highly publicized and widely broadcast attempts at finding the young preteen girl. To this day she's never been found, and with her missing body, we start our count at one.

Next, there was Patrick Dermotty's prime number of nine kills in a single night. Drugging a half dozen of his classmates, his parents and older brother, then disemboweling them with precision and fashioning balloon animals out of their intestines while they watched, drugged and helpless to stop it. There were no balloon therapy sessions for Patrick Dermotty, dubbed the Balloon Boy by the press. The tally grows to double digits at ten. Patrick wasn't alone upon his arrival at Fenton.

In 1980, thirteen-year-old Joseph Giordano burned his adoptive parents and concurrent step-siblings to death in their sleep. But this was only the starting gun. He continued on a clandestine killing spree, killing a mom and pop shopkeeper and a dozen passengers on a charter bus. Giordano enjoyed some regional fame as a child chess phenom, and it's still unknown why he snapped. Much like the Balloon Boy, Giordano hasn't spoken in close to thirty years. He sits in his room, bound in a straightjacket, preventing him from self-mutilating. Joseph Giordano's kills added eighteen to the total, making our count twenty-eight. How can you top eighteen?

Well, sit down, friend and hold your narrator's drink, because we've saved the best for last.

Between 1975 and 1986, Satanic serial killer in training Michael Chase killed many small animals. It started as puberty set in. Conservative estimates of the number of animals he sent over the rainbow bridge in his sacrifices top out around a hundred and fifty through five years. Nobody connected the dots until his junior prom. Chase worked at the pizza shop supplying the food for the event. He replaced the mushrooms on the pizza with deadly redcaps, poisoning thirty-seven of his classmates. Two of his peers garnered special attention. As a result, the sixteen-year-old boy was sent to Fenton under the care of Dr. Pennoire's staff. He mumbles to himself in a corner all day, bobbing his head to and fro.

Depending on how you skin the numbers, Mr. Chase's antics bring our total well into triple digits, passing two hundred souls silenced by only four people.

And now one of them, the Balloon Boy, has been set free ...

"Son of a fucking bitch!" Dr. Pennoire shouted as she slammed her fist into the wall. The vibration caused a glass knick-knack to fall off its shelf and shatter on the floor. Pennoire watched the pieces scatter. She regained her composure and left the crime scene, joining her team.

CHAPTER 5

MELISSA & CLARENCE

FRIDAY, JUNE 11, 2021, 6:25 P.M.

"Yes, we'll be back in port tonight and flying out to JFK on the overnight right away. We should be back at the property by Sunday morning. Thank you," Melissa Dark said, speaking into her cell phone before ending the call. She stood on the deck of the Royal Caribbean cruise ship, staring at the screen. The glare of the bright sun made seeing the phone's touch screen an impossible task. A fresh breeze, salted by the ocean's water, blew her auburn hair into her mouth, sticking to her cherry red lipstick. She brushed it aside with the flick of her free hand. Both hands looked older than her face.

"What was that all about?" Clarence asked, his attire embraced the stereotype he projected: the typical middle-aged, American male tourist. He was stocky, with short blond hair in camouflage shorts, Nike Air Monarchs, and an obnoxious Hawaiian shirt to match his demeanor. All he needed was a selfie stick and a cooler of PBRs to complete the costume. They were in his state room.

"The State Police in New York." Clarence stepped back, his face turning red. "Apparently Ronnie isn't in cell phone range yet and they were trying to reach him too. The Balloon Boy Killer escaped from his mental institution upstate."

"The who escaped from the what?" Clarence furrowed his eyebrows.

"The house in the Catskills, don't you remember? It was a murder house. That's why Ronnie bought it, so he could record that fucking record and that creepy fucking song about the murders there. 'Full Balloon,' remember?"

"Yeah, I hate the fucking song. Brodie wearing the wrestler's mask on stage when he sang the song was fucking ridiculous. I was pissed when he bought that place. I just got settled down in L.A., and then what was it, two weeks of getting the harmonies just right on that motherfucker?" He flicked a toothpick into the ocean. "I told Steve-Bro to catch a cold so he could sing in key. God he was an awful singer. We woulda been bigger if he didn't suck so bad."

"I remember that," she laughed as she replied, the memory bringing her back to a better time, "I hate it there. I can't wait to sell it. It's because of things like this. I have to laugh; the police wanted to warn us to lock the doors on the house. Fenton is two hundred and fifty miles from the Catskills. What's he going to do? Hitchhike? I doubt he stole a car. He was like ten years old when they locked him up, so I don't think he knows how to drive. I'm sure they'll catch him on the local playground bobbing back and forth on a see-saw or something."

"And drinking Kool-Aid?" Clarence snorted in amusement. "If I ever see another packet of Lime green Kool-Aid again, I swear to God I'll kick a small animal."

"You and me both, baby. Let me call Ronnie, see if he made it back to cell phone range and fill him in on what's happening."

"You know, if I know Ronnie, after all that went down, he sees you are calling, he won't answer the fucking phone."

"That's fine. If he doesn't, I'll call Brodie too

and see if he can call him or swing by the house."

"That Amish looking motherfucker still lives out there? Betcha he's building barns and has a horse and buggy."

"Yes, he does; I mean no, he doesn't," Melissa stumbled over her words as she affirmed. "You know what I mean. He lives there. And he has a car. He'll be able to check in, I'm sure."

"That's good. Because he's not going to be happy when he finds out what we did. Motherfucker isn't my biggest fan." The feeling was mutual. Clarence felt nothing but contempt for Steve Brodie and blamed him for the band's break up. He was the one who talked Ronnie into the Loch Ness Monster, or whatever the fuck stupid thing it was, concept album nobody gave a shit about. Next stop, they were playing half-filled clubs and fighting with bar owners for their retainer. It all ended the night Clarence threw his drum stool at Brodie on stage. The next day, the label terminated their contract and ended their tour.

"It's okay, baby. We have to do what we

have to do to make us happy. Ron wasn't around, always on cruises working, right?"

"Right."

"It was worse than him being on the road back in the day; at least then I could go with. Now ..." she hesitated for a moment, "well, we saw what happened."

"Yes, we did. Or at least Ron did."

"He did it to himself."

"He sure did." Clarence Allan held Melissa close, kissing her hard and deep. The ocean waves slammed into the cruise ship's hull, beating in time with their hearts.

CHAPTER 6

PATRICK & JAMEY

FRIDAY, JUNE 11, 2021, 7:16 A.M.

Patrick took the mask and a razor-sharp carving knife and ran from Katie's house in Fulton, New York, just outside of the police dragnet. His goddess guided him. He blended into the brownfields littering the cityscape, avoiding automobiles. Following a river, he came upon the train tracks of the CSX rail yard and waited in the darkness. Soon a train came, and Patrick hopped on the first rail car to come by. He sulked back into the train car, hidden from any onlookers. There, he was able to gather his thoughts as he settled in for the two-hundred-and-fifty-mile trip south.

He was finally free. After all the decades Saint D'Inana told him he must wait, told him he would know when the time was right to complete his quest. And thus he waited, as the moons changed and the flowers bloomed and the snow bit in a never ending cycle of light and darkness. He waited in silent meditation, enduring the enemy's constant interrogations and torture, following the direction of the guards when prompted, gaining their trust. He waited for six thrice six to beckon him on the day of his becoming, when his power would return and guide him once again.

And now the time has come.

He saw Saint D'Inana through the stars, hovering before the moon. This night, his jailers presented themselves to him as sacrifice and opened the gates for his release. He would show no prejudice; he would liberate their souls from this earthly plane, freeing them to fly to be one with Saint D'Inana. A tear of joy came to his eye. Now he could honor Saint D'Inana and finish his quest. He was going home.

Sleep overtook Patrick, taking him places as it always did. The gentle pattern of steel rolling across iron blended into the roar of a crowd ...

•

Nine hours later, Patrick felt the pull of Saint D'Inana grow with each passing minute. He exited the train and went forth into the wilderness. The trees, the earth, the water, all smelled different. They were reminiscent, bringing Patrick back to his youth, so many decades ago. He knew he was close to where the sword lay hidden for decades. He started the long walk to his former home through the forest and rolling mountains of the Catskills.

The sun hung high in the sky and the early summer heat was humid. Black flies, mosquitoes, and no-see-ums bit and punished Patrick as he made his way through the low brush of the Catskills. He didn't swat them away, oh no. He let them feast. It was proper penance for the prize he would soon claim for his own. He felt the pull of Saint D'Inana. It drew him from the trainyard into a gulley. At its base, a small building made of wood and corrugated aluminum stood next to a large drainage outlet. A light came from within, leaking through the cracks in the dwelling's makeshift shell.

Patrick pulled the knife out of his belt and

adjusted the mask covering his face.

•

Inside the rickety shack, just outside the Ulster County CSX Railyards, Jamey Lowe was hard at work in his makeshift lab. The meth cook was putting together another batch. He wore pajama pants, fuzzy slippers, and his club leather vest. Lynyrd Skynyrd filled the earbuds attached to his phone; "Tuesday's Gone" was the current soundtrack. He loved the music, and it helped to drown out the trains.

Jamey's taste in attire always gave others a moment of pause. They found it surprising for a man resembling Judas Priest's Glenn Tipton in any number of 80s hair metal videos to wear jammy pants to work. But Jamey did so. He also knew when you made a meth lab, you needed to put it in the most obscure place possible.

So why not stick it in an abandoned storm drain near the CSX rail yard? It was early summer, and the County stopped using it years ago. There was no reason to fear it flooding out. Come winter, it would have to be shut down from the cold maybe, but until then, it was pumping out a cash crop. So he'd wear jammy pants if he wanted to.

A fresh roast beef sub from the local hoagie shop, purchased earlier, called to him. He broke away from his chores to take a bite or two from the sandwich and saw something in his peripheral vision he didn't like.

Jamey chewed his sub and thought about how much he loved chemistry. His parents couldn't afford college, and as a result, he did the next best thing he could do. He went into the Army to be a Chemical Weapons Specialist. He lived his dream job, and it's also where he started getting into trouble.

He discovered the EM club and five-dollar pitchers of beer. A few years of Article 15s and pay grade reductions left him pissed at Uncle Sam when his time came up. Now an unemployed war vet, Jamey's remaining choices were slim. He soon after hooked up with some bad people who wanted him to make bad things for them. Which he enjoyed doing.

Jamey's fascination with military chemical

weapons grew. His favorite movie? *The Rock*, the Alcatraz affair with his favorite actor, Nicholas Cage. Nick's character was a former Army chemical guy, as was Jamey, a cause for instant bonding with the army vet and the actor. But it bothered Jamey when they used civilian parlance while referring to the chemical weapons used in the movie. There was no such thing as nerve gas, it was a nerve agent.

Jamey had dealt with the deadly compound firsthand while training at the Army's base for chemical weapons in Alabama. As part of his training, he was forced to decontaminate a building the size of an elementary school. One of the guys in his class didn't believe the instructors and took off his mask. They waited to administer the antidote until he started frothing at the mouth and twitching.

All of it was ten years and a war ago. Now, in his spare time from making drugs for his friends, Jamey would make his own versions of CS tear gas and his new favorite, dichloroethyl sulfide, better known as a mustard agent, or gas to the uneducated masses.

First used with catastrophic results in the trenches of World War I, mustard gas emitted a stench reminiscent of horseradish and did horrible things to the human body. Casual skin contact would cause painful blistering. Blindness was almost a sure end result if it got in a person's eyes. If it found its way to the lungs, it would swell and burst the alveoli, causing the unfortunate victim to dry-land-drown in their own blood. He brewed an ample supply of the blister agent, storing it in ampules in the mini refrigerator. And it was the first thing he went for when he heard the first silent alarm go off.

Someone knew he was here, and they were going to pay for it. He threw his colors on the table, the leather vest slid across the surface. Jamey grabbed a section of green PVC tubing and tied it to his back with the strap from his blue terry cloth bathrobe. He took the rack of mustard agent cocktails, grabbed a small duffel bag, and made his way to his safe exit. Whoever it was, he would be long gone by the time they cleaned up the mess and realized where he'd gone. His company was about to wish they never arrived. They ruined his breakfast, the rest of his sandwich sat on the table, and Jamey was pissed he couldn't finish it.

Jamey Lowe slipped down the embankment, almost falling on his ass in the process. His slippers provided little to no traction, and the grass, wet from the morning dew, made the feat nearly impossible. But somehow, he managed to make it down without wiping out. As soon as he reached stable footing, he ran into the wooded lot nestled between the trainyard and Route 287, knowing he wouldn't have much time. As soon as his preventive measures blew, car alarms and sirens would resonate about. This entire area would soon be crawling with every imaginable form of law enforcement seeking the perpetrator of a chemical agent attack.

Jamey had prepared for such a circumstance and hid his bike in an accessible location for an escape. A ramshackle lean-to, covered in vegetation and dead branches, sheltered a motorcycle, not your typical biker road hog, but a Suzuki dirt bike made for backcountry trails. Jamey ripped back the camouflage pattern tarp covering the bike. A backpack sat on the seat, and a pair of high-top Chuck Converse sneakers hung on the handlebar, connected and draped over at the laces.

He kicked off his muddy slippers, untied the Chucks, and put them on his feet. He ripped the bathrobe off, pulled a tattered jean jacket out of the pack, and put it on. He needed to pull his long hair out from under the collar. Jamey placed a black safety helmet on his head. The faceplate was a black shield of plexiglass and fiberglass, obscuring his features and giving him the appearance of an outer space hoodlum. He straddled the motorcycle, looked down at the fuel gauge to make sure enough gas sat in the tank to get the fuck out of Dodge, and prepared to kick the machine to life.

Jamey saw a black shape standing before him.

"What the fuck?" he said, the exclamation muffled by his helmet. He was scared stiff; the figure stayed just as motionless and unmoving, staring back at Jamey. Jamey looked down at the dials and meters on the motorcycle, looked back up, and the shape was gone.

"Is that your final answer?"

The words caught him off guard. Was he losing it? It sounded like some washed up celebrity on a gameshow. He felt movement behind him, and spun his head around, finding out too late the helmet blocked his peripheral vision. Something struck at his off leg.

A stab of pain raced up his spine from the appendage. The first thought to race through his brain told him he'd been shot, but the stinging sensation he felt emanated from the length of the limb. His head darted back around, and he saw he hadn't been shot. It was much worse than a gunshot wound.

Instead, something had sliced his leg open from the top of the thigh down to the ankle, stopping just before the top of his Chucks. It was one cut, razor sharp and deep. At first, he was almost relieved; it didn't look so bad. Then he felt the pajama pants give way and watched in horror as the leg's flesh butterflied open. It was a clean cut; at first, he could see the bones of his leg, curiously, and he marveled at the sight for a moment. He was mesmerized before fully realizing what happened to him.

Blood erupted from the open wound, interrupting the intimate moment he was having, gazing at the bones of his femur and shin. Blood sprayed his helmet, blacking out his vision. He ran out of time to wonder what happened, eliminating his window to scream. Even if he had, it would have been quieted by his helmet.

He fell over, and the bike followed, pinning him by one leg to the spot. Massive blood loss was playing tricks on his mind. A shape in a black mask with blacker eyes, hovering, taunting him as he bled out on the ground. Jamey lay in a pool of blood and forest flooring consisting of pine needles, dead leaves, twigs, and moss. He was unable to move.

After a few moments, he felt a tug on his jean jacket, and then another. It became obvious something was attempting to pull him away from the dirt bike and the lean-to into the foliage. He tried to fight it, but he'd lost too much blood from the cut on his leg and was having trouble keeping his eyes open.

•

Jamey felt his consciousness return in a fog. He'd dreamt as he slept, for however long it was. In the dream, his life was different. He did his tour in the Gulf War, came out an Army Scout, decorated and a prime candidate for public service as a police officer. His military skills soon landed him in the special forces of the police world, a SWAT team, dealing with chemical agents and tossing tear gas at bad guys.

Dreamworld Jamie found himself a single man who never married, he loved his job and wondered what he would do with himself after he retired. Perhaps he would take up with a private security firm, or maybe he'd finally settle down with a nice nurse and make a family. But neither would be the case today. The fantasy numbed the reality Jamie was enduring as he returned to consciousness.

"What the fuck?" he questioned as he gazed at the unexpected sight of a large masked man aiming Jamey's jerry-rigged bazooka at him. A pair of black, soulless eyes were behind the mask. Jamey wished himself back to the dream world where he was a twenty-five-year veteran of war and peace and a month from his retirement.

"I'm sorry, that's the wrong question. The correct question was, 'What is fucked?' and I'm afraid that will cost you."

The meth cook didn't understand what this person was saying. He was still trying to comprehend between the real world and the dream world when he heard a whooping sound followed by a brief whistle and a ding as something metal bounced off the wall behind him. He looked over and saw a trail of smoke in the air. His eyes followed it to a small, smoking canister.

"Survey says! Gas! Gas! Gas!" he heard the same someone shout like they were the announcer on a game show.

Then the earth moved. Jamey felt his ears popping as the air decompressed from a massive explosion. He was already disoriented, but he knew what the invader did. The telltale stench; something smelled funny. At first, he couldn't quite place the foreign odor. It was somewhere between a skunk and rancid, rotting vegetables. The stench kicked his memory awake, and Jamey knew. His mind went through all the possible vectors.

What was it? Rotten horseradish? Sulfur? No.

Mustard Agent.

He turned around to see a yellowish growing and expanding cloud. His arms and face were covered with bleeding sores. The yellow cloud danced about in the room and touched Jamey's cheek, giving him a good whiff of the chemical compound. It burned his skin and nose straight through to the bones in his face. His throat and lungs were on fire. Jamey was unable to move or catch his breath. He tried avoiding the spreading cloud, coughing and gagging, but it soon engulfed him in a jaundiced haze. His thoughts became less and less coherent as the pain ripped through his body. He managed to stand and the cloud covered his body in agony. He let gravity grasp his body and pull him down. He hoped it didn't hurt as much if he was on the ground; maybe the gas would be hovering above it, like smoke from a house fire.

Jamey was wrong as it turned out; the chemicals were concentrated there. He took one final gasp of air and tried to hold his breath as the mustard agent burned and blistered his lungs. The pain finally stopped as Jamey Lowe drowned in his own blood.

•

After he watched the man blister and choke to death, Patrick left the lab. On the way out, he tripped Jamey's countermeasures. Patrick wouldn't have known the lab was rigged. Jamey Lowe set up a half dozen claymore mines about the shack and lab, connected to a motion detector. Patrick possessed no knowledge of them either, nor did it matter. He would be gone soon.

Jamey's motorcycle laid in the dirt outside the shack. Patrick prayed to Saint D'Inana to show him the way, but he never rode a motorcycle before. How could he now? Patrick's foot knocked against the helmet on the round. He picked it up.

Yes. Saint D'Inana.

He put Jamey's helmet on over his mask, stared at the motorcycle ...

And he knew.

Saint D'Inana's essence was trapped, but she could still guide her servant.

He stood the motorcycle up and sat on it. Though he never drove a motorcycle or in his life, his faith in Saint D'Inana guided him. Patrick drove off the county road, following his instinct. Following the scent of the dark goddess.

He was a few miles away when the five-minute timers expired on the landmines. The demolitions blew in unison. The Army vet, along with the lab and any evidence of Patrick Dermotty's presence, ceased to exist in an instant. A lethal cocktail of corrosive chemical compounds, ball bearings, and explosives vaporized everything in their path before any living, or dead, being's brain could register something horrible happened.

The motorcycle's gas tank was full. Following side roads, the motorcycle took Patrick to within a few miles of his old home before he abandoned it in a ditch, the tank half full.

CHAPTER 7

RONNIE & THE CORVETTE

FRIDAY, JUNE 11, 2021, 10:30 P.M.

R onnie Dark sat at the kitchen table, a notepad before him, chewing on a ball point pen cap. He stared at the paper, afraid to write the words. He started to second guess his motivations. He lost his job, his wife, his luggage, and his house. Luggage was luggage; it would come back to him at some point. He could get another woman; those were easy. A job and a roof over his head, they were a bit more pressing in the current economy.

How would he do any of this? Could he get another gig? At fifty years old, he wasn't the kind of guy in demand. Without a gimmick, he was just another washed up guy from a one hit wonder hair metal band. The music world had changed since his prime. Sure, he got royalties from the old label, but they became less and less as each year passed. People were forgetting The Dark, which meant people were forgetting Ronnie Dark.

Without a place to live, getting a new job would be even more difficult. He felt the anger coming back. His hand shook as the pen greeted the paper. Paul Revere, though, he never changed, and he kept playing in the background. Mark Lindsay's lyrics reminded Ronnie he was just like him. He focused on the job at hand.

Dear Bitch, he wrote, then stopped. He ripped the paper off the pad, crumpled it, and tossed it into a nearby trash bin. It joined a dozen other attempts he'd made in the past hour. Why was it so hard to write a suicide note? Robert E. Howard did it easily enough prior to blowing his brains out with a .380 Colt eighty years before.

"All Fled, all done, so lift me on the pyre, the feast is over and the lamps expired." The writer left the paraphrased lines from Viola Garvin's "The House of Caesar" in his typewriter.

Then, bang! All because his mother died.

The manner in which he would end his

own life was yet to be determined. The ways to take your own life were prolific. So, in lieu of writing his suicide note, Ronnie first compiled a list from which he could narrow down his choice of euthanasia. He wrote *Dead List* across the top of the paper in big bold letters, followed by his options:

Gun
Slit Wrists
Hanging
Pills
Carbon Monoxide
Drowning
Fire
Suffocation

Ronnie owned a gun, a big WWII relic, an M44 Russian rifle. It fired a huge bullet, a .30 caliber 7.62 54R round. The rifle was about four feet long, with a sixteen-inch-long collapsible bayonet. The blade was a spike. He thought he might be able to use the rifle to blow his fucking head off. The rifle in question would do the job. But no, no guns. Ronnie's vanity, still present despite having his world turned upside down, wanted an open casket. No, He'd have to do it another way. He crossed

Gun off the list.

He could cut his wrists in the bathtub. He heard exsanguination was a quiet and easy way to go; you just drifted off to sleep in the water, never to wake again. Except there was one problem. Ronnie was scared to death of knives and knew he couldn't bring himself to cut his own wrists. And wasn't there a certain way you cut the wrist? Was it up the arm? What if he missed the vein? No on *Slit Wrists*.

Hanging was an option. The house was designed with plenty of high ceilings, offering a plethora of spaces to tie a rope. But he wasn't confident in his noose tying skills. He'd heard too many stories about people who didn't break their necks in hanging and asphyxiated during a slow, agonizing, and painful death. The mental image of him dangling from the ceiling formed in his mind, thrashing about as piss and shit dripped down his pant leg. The thought of this sent a shiver up his spine. This wasn't happening, and neither was *Hanging*.

There were always pills. But how many should he take? And what kind? Did they even have the pills he'd need to take in the house?

Should he mix them with booze or other drugs? Would they work, or would they just make him sick? Not to mention Mark Lindsay's voice looped in the jukebox in Ronnie's mind, telling him over and over how hard it was to find kicks. The more he thought about it, the less he liked the idea, and he scratched *Pills* off the list.

Carbon monoxide poisoning allegedly put you to sleep and left you as a nice plump and rosy corpse. It smelled like a sweet cigar, and the car in the garage could provide the poisonous gas, allowing him to nod off and never wake up again. He could do it in the car, sure, but it wouldn't be as shocking as him piping the gas into the house, so she could find his body in the living room as she walked in. Yes, Ronnie nodded and poked the word with his pen. He underlined it. *Carbon Monoxide* was a *Dead List* potential contestant here.

How could he drown himself? Ronnie pondered this one for a moment. There was an above ground pool in the backyard; he presumed he could weigh himself down and swim with the fishes. But again, it ruined the effect of her finding him in the house, and she could replace the pool if she wanted. No, he wanted where he died to have a permanent impact on her. He'd remain firm on the rules here. *Drowning* was eliminated.

Fire was crossed off without a second thought on the matter. The reasons not to use fire as an option were plentiful, some for the same reasons as the others he'd thought against. First off, he didn't want to burn the place to the ground, no. And as much as it would be taking the house away from her, she'd get the insurance money, something he couldn't allow to happen, nope. He couldn't trust a controlled blaze, either. Plus, burning to death wasn't known as a preferred method of making it to the other side.

Suffocation could work, he mused. The old plastic bag over the head and duct tape around the neck, then duct taping your wrists to a stairwell banister or other immovable object to prevent removal of the bag. He stopped and thought about it for a moment. He imagined this, too, would be as terrifying a way to go as hanging without breaking your neck. He'd probably thrash about on the floor in spasms before dying and didn't want fear as his final thoughts. No, he wanted his final thought before dying to be *Fuck you, Melissa!* He wrote it on the page and crossed off *Suffocation.*

Carbon Monoxide it would be.

He ripped the *Dead List* off the notepad, set it aside, and found inspiration for his vile, misogynistic suicide note. He didn't care. She deserved every word he wrote. The big, circular clock hanging over the fireplace ticked, reflecting in the windows.

•

A coiled garden hose and a roll of silver duct tape sat on the hood of Ronnie Dark's 1979 Corvette Stingray. The keys were in the ignition, but the car wasn't running, not yet at least. It soon would be; the airplane engine under the car's hood would fire up, the combustion would create an exhaust of lethal carbon monoxide.

Ronnie stuffed one end of the garden hose into one of the 'Vette's exhaust pipes and duct taped the rubber to the chrome. He yanked on it a couple times to ensure it would hold. It did. He uncoiled the hose, running its length to the garage's entrance into the home proper. He opened the door and set the end of the hose on the floor, duct taping it down. He closed the door to the spot where the hose prevented it from latching and sealed the gap with more of the duct tape.

His cell phone rang. He looked down, saw it was Melissa calling him. Calling him like this took some fucking nerve. He thought about answering it, then disregarded the thought. He opted instead to watch her name on the screen and listen to the chirping sound of the smartphone. She'd get a message from him soon enough.

Satisfied with his handiwork, Ron fired up the Corvette's hundred and ninety-five horsepower engine. It roared to life, deafening him in the confines of the garage. He waited a few moments to make sure it would continue to idle. It did. Ronnie opened the bay door and closed it behind him before making his way to the front door of the house. Taped to the door was his suicide note. He was fond of this little twist, playing on the legal papers he found on the door earlier in the day. He poked the note with a finger, then let himself in, locking the door behind him.

Ron felt something new, something he hadn't felt in some time. He was content knowing this would all be over soon. His depression turned to acceptance of what he was going to do. He kicked his shoes off and flopped on the couch. He could hear the Corvette's engine humming in the house, and the slight, sweet taste of the car exhaust filling his home.

The phone rang again; it was Melissa. She was persistent. He assumed she wanted to make sure he understood he needed to be out by Monday. Oh, he'd be out by Monday, he was sure of it.

Don't worry, bitch, I'll be out, don't you worry one bit, Ron thought as he turned his phone off and tossed it across the room. It skipped across the floor and crashed into a corner. He wouldn't need it anymore. Ronnie Dark closed his eyes and drifted off to sleep with a smile on his face, knowing he wouldn't wake up again.

And he was okay with it.

CHAPTER 8

PATRICK & MASON

FRIDAY, JUNE 11, 2021, 11:00 P.M.

Patrick trudged on through the wilderness, snapping tree limbs and dead branches as he went through the miles, led by instinct. He was careful not to trip on the tree roots and clumps of wild grass. The terrain became more familiar, the smell of his youth tickled his nose. The crisp scent of the regional vegetation spurred memories. Maple, birch, and ash trees, golden rod and sumac all blended forming an aromatic cornucopia. The scent remained when the sun set and darkness returned.

Patrick smiled, his joy hidden by the mask he wore. He knew he was close; he could feel Saint D'Inana's presence. She guided him, led him on his way. He reached the pinnacle of a hill and saw it through the trees before him. The house. It sat in the dark, quiet and still, a halo of moonlight glimmering about its frame. Patrick felt his pulse quicken, his heart beat faster in anticipation of what was to come.

Saint D'Inana awaited him.

He picked up his pace and hurried down to the property. The place looked almost the same as when he left thirty-five years ago. The tree line had grown some, the house's stain had faded some more, but everything else remained the same. Patrick crept along the edge of the long driveway, ensuring he was hidden in the shadows of the trees. He passed near the garage and stopped. The rumbling sound of a running engine emanated from behind the closed bay door. Patrick was cautious; he didn't have the luxury of being discovered. He held no knowledge of the new owners, how many people might be in the house. Once he acquired Saint D'Inana, then he could dispatch whoever might be in the home.

Saint D'Inana, his dark goddess, was his main priority. She was near. He shook in anticipation of the reunion. Anxious as he was in the hours leading to this point, Patrick knew once he held Her in his grasp, all would be well.

He peeked in through one of the two

windows built into the bay door. A car, a silver Corvette, hummed away, idling in the garage. He watched for a few minutes, waiting for someone, anyone, to come into the garage and drive off in the vehicle. None came. Satisfied the car wasn't leaving and he wouldn't be seen, Patrick made his way into the back yard.

He passed the above-ground pool. He remembered his father complained about having an above ground pool, the dumbest invention known to man. But the ground on the property was too ridden with tree roots; it could pose a problem when digging for a pool. It's why the house was built on a concrete slab with no basement, and the shed in the backyard, aside from the garage, was the closest thing to storage on the property. To his surprise, Patrick found the shed was wide open. Stocked racks of tools and a table graced the interior.

"I'll take door number one!" he said.

Patrick grasped a rack of tools and slid it aside. A soft clanging of metal on metal answered the action. Though sound was a slight tinkle outside the shed, inside the ringing resonated. He stopped in place until the sound abated. Patrick looked about to see if he'd been discovered. He saw no one.

The floor of the shed was plywood and panel. One piece was darker than the rest. Patrick found a flat head screwdriver on the rack he'd just moved and pried at this piece of flooring. It popped up, revealing a cache under the shed. He reached his hand in, his fingers raking the cobwebs. It was empty.

How could this be? His memory didn't fail him. He put it under the shed, the shed he now stood in. He tore up the flooring around the cache. There was nothing there. Nothing. How could it be? In a fit of rage, Patrick pulled down the tool rack, sending the implements clattering to the ground. A scrub slasher landed on the floor, blade first. It vibrated on impact, the semi-curved metal making a brief warble on impact.

A moving shadow caught Patrick's attention and he slid behind the shed. It provided enough cover to hide his bulk from anyone looking into the backyard. Peeking around the corner, he watched as a pair of headlights snaked up the long, curvy driveway. Patrick felt the draw of the sword, the will of Saint D'Inana urging him to find the blade. He pulled the tool out of the flooring.

•

Working for JFK Airport's Baggage Return Department, bringing late luggage to hapless travelers was the easiest job Mason Pilot ever possessed. There were several reasons he loved this gig, the first job he'd held for longer than three months. He got to drive around all day, dropping off errant bags while listening to whatever he damn well pleased. With his prolific tattooing covering his wrists and face, Mason was thankful he was employed. Plus it paid twenty-five bucks an hour, allowing Mason the luxury to get more ink more often, on top of paying for rent in Rockaway Beach.

Mason's name was written across the knuckles of his fingers and thumbs on both hands. A tiger graced the backside of Mason's right hand. The left was home to a panther's head. Mason loved big predatory cats. A cat paw was on his left cheek. His left arm was a sleeve of tribal rings. A crown of thorns Jesus head covered his right bicep. Mason liked to use the tattoo as an ice breaker, declaring no matter where you were in the room, his divine ink was watching you.

Today the powers that be sent him driving upstate into the Catskills, bringing lost bags home to rich, suburban New Yorkers who worked in the big city but pretended they lived in the woods. The Catskills were populated, a giant backyard rural suburb to the Five Boroughs. As a result, the area spread out what would be half a day's work in the city into a twelve-hour affair. He didn't care; overtime was part of the job, not to mention, pay for O.T. was time and a half. He'd been making almost forty dollars an hour since the sun went down while listening to Linkin Park so loud in volume, his ears rang. And loving every moment.

Mason's last delivery was deep in the woods off Route 28A. Once he was done for the night, he'd take his time driving back to his place in Jersey. The driveway was long and winding, the house was hidden far off the main drag. It was a huge place; the delivery man always marveled at what a ton of money could buy you. He looked at the receipt for the delivery and wondered what Ronald Dick did for a living. With a surname like Dick, Mason first theorized he must be a salesman. Judging by the size of the mansion, Ronald Dick's mental image transformed into a doctor. Or maybe a lawyer; there was no way around it.

Mason parked his blue Caravan in the small parking lot adjacent to the house. He walked into the back of the van; it was empty except for two suitcases, both belonging to Mr. Dick. The delivery man slid both to the back and opened the door. He checked them off his manifest, hanging on a clipboard attached to the van's wall. He hopped out the back, picking up a bag in each arm.

That's odd, Mason thought. There was complete silence outside. No chirping insects, nothing. It made him uneasy. He smelled something in the air. It raised the pinprick-sized roots of the shaved hairs on his tattooed arms. He stood still, trying to shrug off the uncomfortable feeling, but it wouldn't leave him.

He hiked one bag over his shoulder and dragged the other behind him on wheels. He brought them up the steps of the porch, placed the bags next to the door, pressed the white doorbell button, and left. Company policy was to deliver the bags and be done with it. Mason rang the doorbell out of courtesy, even though it was after midnight. He turned, saw a vehicle was coming up the driveway.

Perfect timing, he thought as he walked down the steps of the porch and returned to his delivery van. His job was done. He fired up the engine, Linkin Park picked up where they left off, and Mason Pilot started his long drive home to Queens.

·

The feeling of dread crept up Mason Pilot's spine. His mind was lost in thought, trying to think of anything except the last drop off. His eyes zoned on the road in front of him. The oncoming vehicle broke Mason from his trance. Its high beams were lit up, blinding Mason. He almost hit the SUV as it streaked past him.

"Fuck you, man!" Mason said and gave the red lights in his rear view mirror the finger.

Little dots, the remnants of the lights, swam in the air, floating around the red lights like UFOs. The distraction was long enough. When his eyes returned to the driveway, he saw something standing in the center of the lane. Was it a deer? A man? A bear? His mind never got the opportunity to decipher the information provided. It happened too fast. Mason's instincts cranked the wheel of the van hard left as he slammed on the brakes.

The front left tire of Mason's van blew out, and the centrifugal force tipped the van onto its roof, sending it careening into a deep drainage ditch running parallel to the mansion's private drive. The upturned vehicle slammed into a tree before coming to a stop, ejecting Mason's bucket seat through the windshield. The blow to his head knocked Mason Pilot out cold. A fallen tree's root bed stood tall, an imposing, natural barrier. The wooden tendrils laced together sods of dirt. The impractical projectile slammed into this wall of earth and roots, perpendicular to the ground, some five feet below. It stuck there, its unconscious occupant dangling upside down, and Jesus watched the whole thing.

CHAPTER 9

PATRICK & BRODIE

FRIDAY, JUNE 11, 2021, 10:50 P.M.

There were ghosts on the highway this night. They shifted and swayed with the curves of the road in hues of white, orange, and yellow, brought to life by a pair of headlights. A red Jeep Grand Cherokee SUV cruised down Watson Hollow Road, known as County Route 42 to firemen and police. The vehicle's high beams lit up the surrounding forest, reflecting off the painted lines and signs.

Inside, the Jeep's occupant was a singing fool. It was Steve Brodie, or simply Brodie, The Dark's former lead singer. Ronnie's best friend since he was Ronnie Dick and Brodie was Steve Brudzinzski. He sang along with a version of himself from thirty years before. Back then he was forty pounds lighter, his hair was long and straight, and his beard was thin and close to his face. He heard Jesus is staring at you jokes through most of his tenure with The Dark. Now, with a fuller belly and thicker beard, assholes like Beaver said he looked Amish. Brodie more likened his transformation to that of Jim Morrison or even Van Morrison. One day he was Greek, the great god Pan, frolicking about the forest, having a good old time. The next day he was Roman, a fat ass Bacchus, sitting back and drinking more than his share of wine. Or Kool-Aid, as the case could be.

"Drink the Kool-Aid!" the chorus to "Full Balloon," the song he wrote in the murder house with Ron all those years ago. He hummed along with the guitar riff, tapping his fingers on the steering wheel in time with Beaver's drum beat and Lightning's, God bless his dead soul, bass line.

Brodie braked, and the SUV slowed as it rolled up to the hidden driveway, marked by a pair of red reflectors. He cranked the wheel with both hands and turned off onto the private road. Brodie always hated the driveway leading up to Ronnie's house. Tonight he hated it even more, knowing it was at Melissa's behest.

She had called him, frantic, earlier in the day. Melissa filled Steve in on the divorce and insisted he go to the house to warn Ronnie about the Balloon Boy escaping. At first, the singer wondered how this was his problem. He resigned to his proximity to the Dark house. He was the closest person Melissa knew of.

As it happened, Brodie bought a place in nearby Kingston, New York at the same time Ronnie signed the deed for the Balloon Boy Murder House. He considered Ronnie his best friend, but he also enjoyed living his own private life outside the band. Living near his friend and having a place to escape to within a reasonable drive was a perfect arrangement. Brodie stuck around the area after the band fell apart, opening a profitable local radio station. Ron was still his friend.

"Brodie," she begged him, trying to sound as sweet as she could, "please, can you just take a drive over there and warn Ronnie? He's not answering his phone, and I've been calling him nonstop. The police are certain this Balloon Boy Killer is still upstate; he can't drive and roadblocks have been set up everywhere up here. But just to be safe, can you please go there?"

Maybe he's not answering the phone 'cause you kicked him out? Or, why am I doing this, just so you can rub in the fact he's got to be out before you come back home? Why don't you ask fucking Clarence to do it? Fat chance of that happening! He snickered at the thought of the latter. These and so many other things Brodie wanted to say to her, but he didn't. He held his conceit for her back and remained copasetic.

"Okay, Mel." She hated being called Mel. Brodie never liked her, and always knew she was fucking Clarence, but never said anything because it wasn't his business. The little things he could do to annoy her when provided the opportunity satisfied him some. Even after Clarence's career ending temper tantrum on stage, he kept his mouth shut. "I've got a few things to take care of down here, but after, I'll take a drive up to the house and check in on him."

"Thank you so much, Brodie!"

"It's my pleasure, Mel. I'll let you know."

"This guy killed his nurse; they're saying he made a balloon animal out of her guts, just like before," she replied; now she was ranting, vomiting inaccurate knowledge, and he didn't need to hear it.

"That's what killers do, Mel, they kill people. I've got to go." He hung the phone up before she could drag the call out any longer.

Now here he was, a few hours later, pulling up the long, twisting driveway to Ronnie's house. He hated driving up here; he was always afraid of going off the road and getting stuck in one of the three-foot-deep ditches on either side. A pair of headlights coming from the house came to life, catching Brodie by surprise. He wondered who it might be. Ronnie? The lights grew closer and higher off the ground. A dark minivan Steve didn't recognize came upon him and passed by, inches apart. Brodie watched it pass in the rearview mirrors of his Jeep. The late summer night was pitch black under the canopy of trees encasing the driveway. It was broken by the van's red and yellow caution lights, now fading in the distance. He turned the music up.

The singer made a curious look on his face, chewed his lip, and played with his thick beard.

Who was that? he wondered. It wasn't long before Brodie's questions were answered. As he pulled up to the mansion's parking lot, the lights of his SUV lit the porch and Steve could see some luggage. The small parking lot outside the garage was empty. Cloud cover and trees blocked any ambient lunar light, creating a void dome hovering over the lot.

"Drink ... the Kool-Aid," Brodie repeated, continuing along with the song after the car stereo ended in mid-beat when he turned the SUV off. The interior of the car lit up in response. Brodie opened the door, stepped out of the Jeep. The summer night air was refreshing out here. He found it odd no bugs were biting at his exposed skin as he walked over to the porch. The pair of suitcases sat side-by-side, next to the door. The luggage explained the unmarked van he passed. Poor Ron, the airplane must have lost his bags.

Steve felt a stinging sensation, more than a bug would inflict, along the small of his neck. Something warm and wet dripped down his back.

What the fuck? he thought when his hands

didn't respond to the mental command to inspect the sensation. He tried to scream but couldn't make a noise, exasperated air escaped from his lungs. His legs gave out a moment later, and Brodie fell down the stairs. He was helpless as he fell, banging his head off the steps before face planting on the lot. The resulting impact shattered all eight front incisors in Brodie's mouth while flattening his nose in a bloody mess of displaced cartilage and torn flesh. Dazed, he was disoriented and found himself staring at the front tire and rim of the Jeep, the blacktop cold against his cheek.

Unable to move or do a damn thing about what was happening except view it as a bystander, the singer started to panic. Brodie wondered if he experienced a stroke or some other medical abnormality. A stroke would have paralyzed one side of his body. It also didn't explain what was wet on his back. When two nondescript work boots covered in mud and pine quills came into view, Steve knew this wasn't a health issue. Someone did this to him.

Steve Brodie blamed his bad luck. It was

the Balloon Boy, of course. The cops were wrong, and Melissa sent him to his death. With his presence, there was no question Ronnie was dead, so his trip up here didn't need to happen.

Brodie knew what was coming next. He had studied Patrick Dermotty's history when writing "Full Balloon." The singer's belly was destined to be cut open, followed by Dermotty's removal of Brodie's intestines. As he bled out, the Balloon Boy would make something resembling an animal out of the offal. He wondered what critter the killer would craft; a dog or a cat? Would he live long enough to see the final product? Or would he bleed to death first from the massive hemorrhaging associated with disembowelment? Brodie supposed it didn't matter.

"Do you want what's behind door number one, door number two, or door number three?" he thought he heard Monty Haul say. He must be hallucinating from the blood loss. "Let's make a deal!"

The sensation of being lifted gave Steve Brodie vertigo. He didn't feel his assailant grab him, but he sure felt the world spin. Brodie's head slapped off the person's back end, bobbing and swinging about in the process.

"Door number three it is!" The words from the phantom announcer faded as the singer watched his Jeep and the parking lot disappear before he lost consciousness.

•

Patrick finished his responsibilities in the pump house, stood before it, and smiled. The moon shone down upon him, turning his masterpiece black in the lunar light. It was a glorious display, the gifts he left for his dark goddess. He could feel Saint D'Inana's pride in his work flow through his veins. It made him shiver with anticipation of their imminent reunion. She grew stronger; he felt this too. One more sacrifice, he resolved, should be sufficient to bring Saint D'Inana back to him. He walked back to the garage.

Inside, the Corvette hummed away, idling in place. Patrick entered the garage through the side door, closing it behind him. Tonight's offerings to Saint D'Inana were placed as desired by the will of his dark goddess. She promised Patrick there would be enough souls to bring her to this world. This meant there would be more sacrifices to Saint D'Inana this night. Each offering made Saint D'Inana stronger and helped him find her.

He held the scrub slasher, ready to strike, its blood-soaked wooden handle black with gore. He searched for whomever left the car running. But no one was in the garage. A hose ran from the car to a door. Patrick cut the hose; the two ends fell to the garage floor with a slap. He looked in the car; there was no one. He looked around the car, under the car. Still he found no one. He could sense Saint D'Inana's presence. As with anything regarding his dark goddess, it wouldn't be easy to find her. After all, he had waited for her to call him home through almost four decades. Now he was here, and the fulfillment of everything he achieved until now would soon come to fruition.

Patrick sat on the garage floor and meditated. It's how he'd talked to Saint D'Inana for all those years. He cleared all the other thoughts out of his mind and left a singularity—Saint D'Inana's image burning with black fire—in his focus. He saw the sword in his mind. The red ruby setting in the blade's hilt, Saint D'Inana's eye, cast a crimson aura about the blade as he concentrated on it.

Could they be ... in the house? Patrick wondered. He opened his eyes and scanned the garage.

He found his vision blurring; something wasn't right. He tried opening the door, but it was locked. Then he realized it wasn't a house door he tried to open; it was a cupboard. He smashed his fist into it, flipping and scattering the wooden shelves and bottles of cleaning agents. The contents crashed to the floor and Patrick fell back into the car's hood. He felt dizzy, turned and saw a full-sized door. He pushed himself off the car, fell forward into the door and turned the knob. He pulled it open and staggered back. Patrick took a step forward, tripped over a bucket and mop, and slammed his head into the wall in front of him. He'd stumbled into a closet. This wasn't what Saint D'Inana told him would happen. He stepped back, turned about, and fell backward, missing the Corvette. Patrick's head slammed into the wall, smashing through the drywall.

His neck hung on the half inch thick gypsum and paper between a pair of framing two by fours. He raised his head and slammed it into a cast iron pipe, hidden in the wall. The blow sent stars swimming through Patrick's brain. He gasped for air with a quick succession of breaths and blacked out, succumbing to the deadly poison of the car's exhaust. Patrick lay unconscious in the garage, hidden by the dark and shadows. His breathing was slow and shallow, and if someone discovered his body, they'd be sure he was dead.

His body shut down to the essentials, a combination of the toxic carbon monoxide and the blow to his head. His mind was active. The brain is an amazing organ. It's the one device capable of time travel, according to the laws of physics. A human mind can travel back, and some can travel forward, through time. Right now, Patrick's psyche was back there again, in the house so many years ago, retracing his steps. Swirling through his thoughts were three words:

Where's Saint D'Inana?

His dark goddess, the reason he was here. His reason to live. He had carefully placed her under the flooring of the shed those many years ago. He felt her there. He could sense her power was weak and knew with each sacrifice it would grow as she fed on the energy he created for her. He focused on the power feeding her, following its trail. And he found her. In Patrick's dreamworld, it was always the same. He traveled to another place in another time ...

•

He stood in a colosseum, sand covering the floor. A light wind swirled it about, creating a fog of dust. It muted Patrick's vision of the spectacle around him. He couldn't see shit, but he could hear. He was a warrior in an arena fighting for the attention of the Queen of Death, Saint D'Inana. And the masses in attendance adored him, cheering and chanting his name in the tongue of the Saints.

"Candor! Candor! Candor!"

The Saints were fickle deities, a dozen omniscient and often bi-polar cosmic beings overseeing the affairs of mortal men. Known as The Twelve, they were lost to the memories of man long before the modern mythological pantheons came into being. Their lasting impression on the men and women of this Earth led to the legends and myths of the current age. Patrick's dark goddess, Saint D'Inana, was paramour to the Death King of the Saints, Nec'ral. Side by side, they sit before their servant on a throne of bones. At their beckon, wave after wave of dead things enter the arena, snarling and howling for fresh blood. Each is infected by the essence of the Dragon, an infection older than time itself. This isn't a dinner service. Instead, the unholy consorts are delivering them to be cleansed by their hero of darkness.

Patrick is armed and empowered by his dark deities. The gladius he wields, known to the people of this time as Mourning, is the embodiment of his patron Saint of Darkness, D'Inana. His armor, crafted in the form of the dragon, was blessed by his Dark Sire, Nec'ral. While wearing the armor, he was invulnerable and could see through any deception as his Dark Lord willed it.

The wave of dead things rushed forward. Patrick—no, Candor—stands his ground. He holds his sword at guard, ready to strike the first of the horde rushing forward. He swings the blade with all his might, connecting with the first of the corrupted beings. Mourning slices through it, leaving a trail of disintegrating dust behind. It was the same with each and every one to come within reach of the magical bronze blade. With every dispatched being, Saint D'Inana grew in power and strength, thriving in the mayhem. The crowd cheered him along with each blow, audible gasps and aahs coming with each appropriate instance of a spectacular killing moment.

Then, without any prior indication, the waves of creatures stop. The masses observing fall into a hushed silence. There is nothing but the wind. A pair of ravens fly over the arena, and Patrick feels the familiar vertigo returning, as he falls through the cosmos back to the world his body inhabits. The world Saint D'Inana wishes to return to. Sacrifices were required to find where his Goddess was hidden.

Hours passed in the world of men until something pulled Patrick from his toxic slumber. Why did Saint D'Inana bring him back now? There must be someone else for him to feed to his dark mistress.

•

Still buckled in, Mason Pilot sat, dazed staring up at the sky as his head lolled back in the seat. How long he was in the woods, hanging upside down, he wasn't sure. He felt blood, now dried and crusted after streaking down his face from cuts on his head. It was long enough for the sun to come up, this much was certain. The sun glared, taunting him. Sweat and dew mingled on his face, stinging his eyes.

Flies buzzed about him, dive bombing and biting. Mason flailed at them with his hands, but they kept coming.

He could see the wreckage of his van scattered about the area, but he couldn't see the road or the driveway he blew off. The cell phone was in the van, he couldn't call anyone, and the seat belt was jammed, locked in place. Try as he may, Mason couldn't slip out of the seat. He was trapped.

When the bugs stopped biting, Mason noticed. The ambient sounds of the forest followed suit. Mason felt the hairs on his neck raise. He heard something moving behind him, then the sun was blocked out by a masked man hovering over the stunned delivery driver. He held a wicked curved knife with a wooden handle.

"Help me ..." Mason managed.

"No whammies! No whammies! No ..." The man held the knife handle to his mouth like a microphone, stretching the O in no out for a whole breath. "Whammies!"

Then he saw the hooked blade flip around, and he knew this wasn't going to end well for him. The hand raised up and Mason heard a whoosh of air. He felt an impact, but it wasn't on his body. The man cut him from the chair. "Big money!" the man shouted and cheered.

For a brief moment, he was weightless, then gravity took over and Mason Pilot fell to the ground. His head, already tender from a concussion caused by the accident earlier in the morning, didn't hold up well. Mason bounced his skull off the catalytic converter of his delivery van, knocking him back out.

CHAPTER 10

RONNIE & THE ROPE

SATURDAY, JUNE 12, 2021, 7:00 P.M.

The evening sun shining through the bay window in the dining room was bright and crisp. It cut a laser beam over Ronnie Dark's sleeping body, waking him up. Ronnie felt the worst hangover of his life. If he knew anything about the afterlife, he was pretty sure there were no hangovers in Heaven. This meant he must be in Hell. Which didn't surprise him in the least.

Hell resembled his house, much to his disappointment. He rolled off the sofa and fell on the floor. He landed on the fuzzy, padded carpet in the living room. Thankful for the cushion, Ronnie pushed himself up.

He felt the fibers of the carpet stick into the cuticle of his right index finger. They were needles, pricking him. He was getting a hangnail. He put the infected finger in his mouth and sucked on it, attempting to relieve the stinging sensation. He could taste the heat of the infection brewing under the skin, peeling the flesh away from the nail and cuticle. Hangnails sucked. He was in Hell and he was going to have a hangnail for eternity.

Three things were certain. He suffered the worst dry mouth of all time, he was thirsty as fuck, and he was about to pee himself. Ronnie got up and headed to the bathroom. Walking down the hall, he brushed his right hand against the wall, making incidental contact with the hangnail on his finger. He shrieked in pain. It was payment for chewing his fingernails to the quick while he sat in the cruise ship's brig. Add another thing to Melissa's Fuck You Ronnie list.

"Damn, that fuckin hurts. Jesus fucking Christ!" He winced, wondering if he should invoke the Lord's name in Hell. He entered the bathroom; the lid was up and he didn't bother lifting the seat. Ronnie noticed his urine was a dark yellow. He rubbed his lips with his forearm and wrist, wiping off the accumulation of dry mouth crud in the corners of his mouth.

He went back to the living room, saw the hose was still intact, hanging off the edge of the door. It hadn't worked for whatever reason. Ronnie slammed his hand onto the door frame, the impact sent bolts of pain shooting up his index finger from the hangnail infection.

"Son of a fucking bitch!" he shouted, shaking his hand to relieve the pain. "I should be fucking dead. Fuck." He kicked the door to the garage open. The garage was dark except for the light flooding in from behind Ronnie. The Corvette sat quiet, drained of gasoline. The hose lay on the concrete floor of the garage, cut in two pieces. Ronnie picked up the cut hose and inspected it. He threw it down. "Cheap ass made in China Walmart fucking bullshit! The fuck!"

Ronnie opened the door to the car, paying attention to his infected finger. He turned the car over. Nothing. He tried it again with the same result and punched the steering wheel with his left hand.

"Why can't I do a fucking thing right?" He got out of the 'Vette, slammed the door, and this time he caught the hangnail on the handle and screamed in agony. "Is this for fucking real? I can't—" he kicked the car's quarter panel— "even—" he kicked it again— "fucking kill myself—" he pounded both forearms into the car's roof— "without fucking it up!" The metal of the roof indented and popped back up. "The fuck!" He couldn't even drive to the gas station to refill the car to try it again. He thought about calling an Uber or a taxi, but he recalled Melissa locked him out of their bank accounts. Frustration took over Ron's thought process.

The guitarist turned around and stomped back into the house, pulling the doorknob behind him. The door slammed shut, but Ronnie didn't release his grip on the handle. He yanked the aluminum chrome plated knob from the door. The pieces of the handle's mechanism clattered to the floor. He looked at the mess of metal scattered about, shook his head in further disbelief, rolled his eyes, threw his hands to his sides, and walked away.

Ronnie retrieved his cell phone and turned it back on. There were twenty missed calls. All of them were Melissa. His voicemail's inbox was full. Without listening to a single word from Melissa's mouth, Ronnie deleted the messages.

"Give it up, you stupid bitch. I bet Clarence would love to see how you blew my phone up!" He said to the phone and placed it in his pocket. He sat down at the table, put his elbows on it, and cradled his head in his hands, sighing. His mind was a chaos of thoughts. He couldn't focus on anything. Melissa and Clarence, losing the house to her lawyers, getting fired from his job, and all this bullshit. He opened his eyes to find the dead list sitting on the table, staring him in the face. The pen sat next to the pad of paper. Ronnie dropped his right hand onto it, clasping it between his fingers, careful not to abrade the hangnail.

"If at first you don't succeed," he said and sighed. Ronnie tapped the dead list with his pen. The hangnail on his finger was at the apex of where he held his pens and pencils. He knew in advance writing anything at all would be about as painful as it could get.

Why can't anything be easy for me? he wondered, now clicking the pen's retractable point in and out.

He was forced back to the drawing board. Car exhaust and carbon monoxide were a wash. He reviewed the remaining options available.

Gun

Slit Wrists

Hanging

Pills

Carbon Monoxide

Drowning

Fire

Suffocation

Gun, still a no. Ron didn't think he'd be able to pull the trigger on the rifle, leaving a bullet to the head out. He wasn't about to slit his wrists and take a bath. After the car fiasco, he was certain he'd cut his wrists wrong. Melissa would find him half alive, get him to a hospital, save his life, and hold this over him the rest of his years. He could see and hear her now, bent over, Clarence riding her from behind.

"I saved your miserable excuse for a life. Where's my alimony?"

No, he reaffirmed himself, and crossed *Slit Wrists* off, again. The pen pressed against his hangnail and the infected finger throbbed in pain as he crossed off the words. He dropped the pen and sucked on his finger. He felt a slim strip of flesh separating from his cuticle tickle his tongue. Biting into it, Ron peeled the flesh back, stinging him to his core. He yanked his finger out of his mouth and spit the bit of skin out.

"Good fucking God!" Ron exclaimed. The pain subsided for a moment, then increased as the saliva covering it dried and the air stimulated the exposed nerve ends. He shook it off, picked up the pen, and continued narrowing down his options for attempt number two.

Hanging could be doable, he resolved. Sure, it wasn't as go-to-sleep easy as carbon monoxide poisoning, but at least it should be quick. Plus, Ron supposed he couldn't fuck it up. Sure, the chances he'd choke to death rather than break his neck were higher, but at least he'd still be dead before she came home, hanging around like a morbid tree ornament.

He looked around the living area. The thirty-two-foot cathedral ceiling connecting the upstairs bedrooms to the lower living area would be perfect, if he could manage to connect the rope to the chandelier. He second guessed this one right away. No, tying the rope to the railing and dangling in front of the door would be better and more practical. Melissa would open the door and see him swaying, his face most likely black, blue, and bloated with his tongue sticking out.

"We have a winner!" Ron said. He stood up from the table and set out to procure the rope from the shed.

•

The sun set and night returned to the Catskills twenty minutes before anyplace else. The canopy of trees and shadows of the western peaks brought it a premature darkness. In spite of this, Ron could still see the shed was a disaster area. He didn't remember leaving the shed in such disarray. Sure, he was drunk and it was dark when he came out last night to get the duct tape, but he didn't recall being such a slob. The floorboards were broken, too, revealing a crawlspace under the shed he never knew existed. No one noticed it when they moved the shed to accommodate the new pump house for the pool a few years ago. Ronnie bent down, looked in, saw it was empty, and shrugged his shoulders. His finger grazed a shelf as he stood back up, sending a jolt of agony through his arm.

"Fuck you." Ronnie told his finger.

The yellow braided rope he sought hung on a spike, nailed into a stud on the wall. Ron grabbed the spool of nylon, held it in his left hand so as not to irritate the hangnail any further. He could imagine the pain if one of the nylon threads stabbed him in the finger.

Ron's phone rang again. He dug it out of his pocket and scraped his hangnail on the seam of his jeans. He bit his lip and sucked in a deep breath. The stinging pain shot through his hand. He pulled the phone out, looked at the screen, and saw it was Melissa calling, again. His anger rose, knowing he hurt himself because of her.

"Fucking buy a fucking clue! I don't want to talk to you!" Ronnie said and sent the call straight to voicemail. Ronnie shook his head in disbelief, turned his ringer off, and dumped the smart phone back into his pocket. He closed the door to the shed behind him, clasped it, and headed back to the house.

•

The mirrored doors of the medicine cabinet in the bathroom were opened. Various bottles of painkillers, cold remedies, and expired prescriptions lined the shelves. Ronnie located a box of Band-aids and relief washed over his face. He was tired of the pain in his finger.

He selected a medium-sized bandage from the box, opened it, and wrapped it about his torn finger. The guitarist couldn't believe he was about to commit suicide but was forced to bandage up a hangnail in order to complete the task. Fucking hangnails were a life changing event, forcing you to do things you wouldn't normally feel you have to do. He wrapped it tight, the pressure dulling the burning sensation of the infected cuticle. Satisfied with the results, Ronnie closed the vanity's doors and left the bathroom. A short walk down the hall found the loft overlooking the foyer.

An oak banister stood as a barrier between the loft and an eighteen-foot fall to the first floor. The ceiling was another twelve feet above the ledge. Ron didn't think the banister would support his weight, but it could be used as a pulley as well as a platform to drop from. Behind him, an antique, wrought-iron radiator, bolted to the floor and attached to piping, sat under a window. Ronnie tied one end of the rope to the radiator and crafted a slipknot noose to the other end. He threaded the rope through the dowels and wrapped it over the rail.

A kitchen chair sat next to the banister. Ronnie stood on the chair and placed the noose around his neck. He stepped up onto the rail of the banister, teetering until he found his balance. Tears of anger formed in his eyes. Here he was, again. Offering all there was left to give the former love of his life, Mrs. Melissa Dick aka Dark, was Ronnie Dark, born Ronald Richard Dick, Junior, age fifty-one. But she didn't want him. She wanted fucking Clarence.

He stood erect, bobbling on the rail. His

tears were replaced by a grin; the musician raised his arms and gave the front door the finger, times two. This time, he would get to say it, not think it, loud and proud.

"Fuck you both!" Ronnie Dark said, a victorious excitement to his voice. He spit a huge wad of phlegm into the air and stepped off the rail.

CHAPTER 11

MELISSA & YOUTUBE

SATURDAY, JUNE 12, 2021, 11:00 P.M.

Melissa Dark sat in her seat on the Delta Airlines Boeing 737, Flight DL-8787, three rows and an aisle separated from her boyfriend. She missed the days of first class, when she could snuggle to her man on a flight. Now, with social distancing a thing even on airlines, at least she could stretch out.

Clarence, who barely fit in his seat, fell asleep an hour ago. His snoring was irritating the woman closest to him. Melissa turned the volume up on her headphones to drown it out. Now she found herself watching YouTube videos. What else did she have to do? A playlist surrounding the key words Balloon Boy Murder House transformed her phone into a time machine. They told the story; one she was part of. She hit play on the first video and traveled back to 1984 ...

THOMAS R CLARK

Television News Report
October 14, 1984, NBC News Affiliate, Channel 4

A camera focuses on a home. The flashing lights of rescue vehicles are seen. Gurneys carrying sealed body bags to coroners' vans are blurry but recognizable in the background. A reporter, a young man in a cheap suit with dark hair and glasses, steps in front of the camera.

"This is Ron Pesha coming to you live from Ulster County. As you can see, State Police and Ulster County Sheriff Deputies have been called to the home of car salesman Jack Dermotty. It's not known what has happened, but we can report there have been multiple fatalities. The youngest of the Dermotty children was seen earlier being taken away by Child Protective Services."

A smiling picture of Jack Dermotty splashes across the television screen. This is followed by video footage of the family used in advertising. Little Patrick Dermotty with his baseball cap and Hulk Hogan t-shirt, smiling away as he pretends to drive a Chrysler K-Car.

"We'll have more on this later tonight as the story develops. This is Ron Pesha for WNBC. Back to you in the studio, Greg."

The camera cuts away from the live report, back to the WNBC studio.

The app segued into the next video; it's another short news spot from less than a year later ...

Television News Report
January 6, 1985, CBS News Affiliate, Channel 2

A News desk with a trio of anchors comes into view. The recording is grainy. A middle aged woman takes the lead on the story.

"It took the jury less than thirty minutes to decide the fate of Balloon Boy murderer Patrick Donald Dermotty. Dermotty made news last fall after savagely mutilating his family and a group of classmates. Famously tried as an adult, Dermotty's attorneys successfully lobbied for an insanity plea."

The camera cuts to Dermotty's attorney, Marcus Stornelli.

"No judge wants to be known as the judge who sentenced a ten-year-old boy to death. It's bad enough we're locking him up in a nuthouse and throwing away the key."

The camera cuts back to the studio, where the live reporter continues his report.

"Newly elected Ulster County Judge, the honorable William Barrett, sentenced Dermotty to nine consecutive life sentences at Fenton State Hospital for the Criminally Insane, one for each victim. The Balloon Boy Killer won't be eligible for parole until well into the next century. It's unlikely he'll ever see another day of freedom, something that makes me, and the parents of his victims, happy."

The camera cuts to footage of a weeping woman, her husband holding her, a look of despair hangs upon his face.

"He's a monster! He's not human! They better throw that (censor beep) key away!" the husband tells the camera. The news report ends with a pixelated edit.

The next video is preempted with an advertisement for a divorce attorney, of all things. She didn't need one of them anymore, thank you, Google and your advertising algorithm. She skipped the ad. The next video she remembered well, even thirty years later.

Television News Report
August 19, 1987, ABC News Affiliate, Channel 7

A camera zooms in on a large home, errant branches and leafy tree limbs obscuring it. A young woman's voice narrates.

"The Balloon Boy Murder House was sold today, purchased by popular guitarist Ronnie Dark, the man behind popular heavy metal band The Dark. The band has risen to prominence with its breakout album, Room, and the smash hit radio single and MTV music video "Fly." We asked Mr. Dark why he purchased the dilapidated and vandalized mansion located in Ulster County in the Catskill Mountains."

The camera switches to Ronnie Dark, his long brown hair tied off in a ponytail, covered head to toe in black: T-shirt, jeans, and leather.

"I got it for a steal! Plus, it's got a weird

kind of history, you know. The Balloon Boy Killer is famous, a modern legend like Jason or Freddy, but real! I think it adds a bit of atmosphere to the place, gives it character. Plus, I wanted to be near the Big Apple, where everything happens on the East Coast."

Scenes of emergency vehicles surrounding the property and CSI investigators walking about cut to the smiling cherub face of a young boy.

"It was only three years ago this fall that ten-year-old Patrick Donald Dermotty, son of car dealership magnate Jack Dermotty, brutally murdered his father, his mother, Shirley, and older brother, John, Jr., and a half dozen of his classmates. Dubbed the Balloon Boy Killer by the press, Dermotty is alleged to have poisoned his victims before mutilating their bodies. He is currently incarcerated at Fenton State Hospital for the Criminally Insane in Upstate New York."

Footage of Fenton State Hospital fades into a montage of photographs depicting graffiti flashes across the screen.

"The home is rumored to be haunted and has been the subject of many break-ins since the property was vacated. When asked if he would be building a recording studio in the infamous dwelling, Dark had this to say:

Back to Ronnie Dark, smiling, his eyes hidden behind Ray Bans.

"Of course I'll be building a studio here. You never know what the muse, or the ghost of some hacked-up kid, might inspire in the middle of the night. I mean, the Eagles recorded "Hotel California" in a haunted house, didn't they? And that sold a gazillion copies, right? And didn't Black Sabbath record in a haunted castle once or twice? So I guess if The Dark recorded their next album here, it wouldn't be unprecedented. It's kinda exciting, ya know. Hey, you busy tonight?"

The camera cuts to the reporter, a young woman with long red hair and piercing green eyes. She is still blushing from the rock star flirting with her.

"For Eyewitness News 7, this is Katie Stammel. Back to you in the studio, Frank." The camera then fades out on the mansion.

"And there you have it, folks," a man answers in a low baritone, almost the opposite of the reporter's spunk and enthusiasm,

"Ronnie Dark from the band The Dark, settling down in the Catskills. We'll be back with sports right after this commercial break."

Melissa remembered being furious with him for flirting with the reporter, then she fucked Beaver in the garage after Ron fell asleep. She justified it as revenge.

The next video up was the *Unsolved Mysteries* episode featuring the house. She remembered the experience too. The crew made a mess, and someone, a nosy producer, asked too many questions about her friendship with the Dark's drummer.

She noted the battery on her phone was low; they'd be landing soon. She plugged it in and swiped away YouTube as the opening credits with Robert Stack played. Melissa turned the phone off and made herself comfortable in her seat. In a few minutes she was asleep.

CHAPTER 12

PATRICK & JOLENE

152

SUNDAY, JUNE 13, 2021, 3:22 A.M.

Ulster County Sheriff's Deputy Jolene Stevens sipped her coffee and sighed as the hot liquid trailed down her throat. Holding the wheel of her white Charger with one hand, she weaved through the curves of Route 28A to Watson Hollow Road at a constant fifty-five miles an hour. The gold and blue detailing declaring SHERIFF'S DEPUTY streaked like lasers at night. A six-year veteran of the New York State Police before settling down in Kingston with her firefighter husband, Stevens enjoyed the general quiet of the resort area.

Other than serving as gatekeepers to downstate tourists who might get out of hand, her job was pretty easy. A good cup of Joe was the best partner you could ask for. Robberies, stolen cars, and the like were the most common calls. They might have a murder a year, if any at all. The last time the county was intimate in notoriety with the latter was long before Jolene's tenure.

After Deputy Stevens received a call earlier in the morning from the State Police in Onondaga County, she made sure her coffee was extra strong. She was going to need the caffeinated back up. The Troopers believed an escaped lunatic could be in the area, the same lunatic responsible for the all-time high Ulster body count lottery some thirty-five years ago: Patrick Dermotty. Still, she kept her cool and maintained her typical no-nonsense attitude.

Jolene reached the driveway of the Dark mansion and put her coffee cup in the drink holder. She parked her Charger in the lot by the mansion's attached garage. A vehicle already sat there, a red Jeep with New York plates and a regional dealer's plate guard. She ran the number before leaving her car. The truck belonged to a local, Steve Brudzinzski, with a Kingston address. She exited her cruiser, inspecting the property, one hand on her holstered Glock, the other holding a flashlight.

The area was clear. A pair of suitcases sat

on the deck leading to the front door. Jolene found this to be curious, considering the house lights were off and windows covered with blinds. The place looked deserted.

A light caught her peripheral vision. It came from the garage. The deputy walked around to the attached building, saw it dark and empty except for a Corvette. She flashed her light into the expanse of the garage. It was a mess: tools were on the floor, and the door to the interior of the house was ajar, but nothing looked out of the ordinary.

Deputy Stevens moved to the porch and approached the front door and abandoned baggage. She looked for a doorbell button, found it, and went to push it when she heard a loud crash from inside the home. Her demeanor changed from curious to concerned. Jolene drew her pistol and knocked on the door.

"Ulster County Sheriff Deputy!" She commanded. "Open the door!"

There was no response. She put her ear to the door, listening.

Soft footsteps resonated as someone walked down the wooden stairs. She repeated her announcement. The steps continued yet no one answered. She tried the doorknob. It didn't turn. She thought about shooting the lock off but knew it wouldn't work on a security door to a mansion like this place. Instead, she ran off the porch to the garage.

The side door to the garage was a Home Depot special. She threw her shoulder into the door; it didn't budge. She stepped back and kicked at it. The door's frame creaked. A second kick followed; her boot connected with the door. It blew open, snapping back on its hinges and cracking loud into the adjacent wall. Stevens ran through the garage into the house, coming out in the foyer and coat room.

She was greeted with a scene of carnage. Pieces of wood littered the floor. A length of rope trailed across the flooring. Twenty feet higher on the second-floor landing, the remains of a railing and banister stood, a jagged V cut into it. On the floor was an unconscious man, attached to the rope.

She clasped her flashlight to her belt, then clicked on her hands-free radio. She thought she could see the shadow of someone standing at the top of the loft, their features obscured by the lighting. Her eyes must have been playing tricks on her. She blinked and the shadow was gone.

"Dispatch, Charlie zero three, requesting backup and emergency response vehicle to One-Four Hillside Drive," she released her push-to-talk. There was no reply from Dispatch. She repeated her call with the same result, static. She turned her radio off and on twice.

"Dispatch, do you copy?" she asked again, never once losing her composure. Still no reply. Survival instincts kicking in, she thought about leaving the premises. She tried the radio one last time with the same result. Satisfied the man was alive and safe from further harm, the deputy holstered her pistol.

Jolene Stevens made a lot of wise decisions in her life. She kept her chastity until marriage, graduated with a regent's diploma, went to community college straight out of high school. Criminal Justice studies were followed by acceptance to the New York State Troopers. During this tenure, she met her husband, Ted, married him, and when his career called, followed him to Kingston. The deputy broke her wisdom streak, terminally, when she holstered her weapon and tended to the man on the floor.

Jolene knelt at his side. She grabbed his wrist and found a pulse. His neck was bruised red and purple by the rope attached to it. The man groaned. Jolene exhaled a sigh of relief.

"Okay, buddy, you're lucky to be alive," she told him. She pressed the button on her radio, again. "Dispatch, Charlie zero three, do you read me? Over." The radio was always reliable. Until now. She'd have to call them on her phone. She detached her cell from its holster on her belt. Before she could dial, two things she never expected in her years as a peace officer occurred in quick succession.

"I'm sorry, but you already used your phone-a-friend! You'll have to ask the audience," what sounded like a gameshow host whispered in her ear, followed by something else unexpected.

The blow came from behind. There was no pain, but she felt the blade sink deep into her shoulder and lock into the bones. Her phone ejected from her hand and spun across the floor. Instead of screaming, she grunted as instinct kicked in. The veteran police officer fumbled to draw her pistol but found herself kicking her feet in the air as she was tugged backward by whatever hooked her. She would have fallen to the floor, but her assailant grabbed her by the neck. Huge arms encircled her throat, clasping around it, smothering her. Unable to breathe, Jolene saw stars as the blood flowing to her head was cut off. She struggled for a moment before losing consciousness.

CHAPTER 13

MELISSA, CLARENCE & BOB

SUNDAY, JUNE 13, 2021, 8:30 A.M.

Melissa Dark and Clarence Allan stood on the curb of the ride sharing lot at JFK airport, waiting for their Uber driver to show up. A stack of luggage stood next to them on a courtesy cart. Melissa never traveled light. This ride to the Catskills was going to cost them a couple hundred bucks. Clarence resolved Ronnie was becoming a money pit, but sometimes you were forced to spend the money to remove the issue.

It was one more thing to add on to the mountain of shit. The flight was a nightmare. Their plane was forced to make an emergency landing in Atlanta, where they sat on the runway for three hours. He put his hand on their bags and patted them, relieved missing luggage wouldn't be on their list of maladies.

"Have you heard anything from Brodie?"

he asked Melissa. She didn't immediately answer, staring at the app on her phone. A small car icon moved toward their position on the map. "Hey, blondie, did Brodie call you back?"

"Brodie? No. I don't think so." Her eyes were distant, it was apparent her thoughts were someplace else. It became clear where they were as she continued to speak. "You think Ronnie is okay? I haven't heard from him either." Which was true. She'd called at least a half dozen times.

"Fuck if I know. And why do you care anyhow? If he kills himself, it will be one less problem to deal with. Plus, we might be lucky and see an increase in old album sales. It would be good to get a royalty check for once."

"Clarence! How could you say that?"

"He's going to be a pain in our asses until we die, you know that, right?"

"But he doesn't deserve to die."

"If—and this is a big if—if this fucking murderer is there and he kills Ron, he did it! We didn't. So what if our plan caused it? I don't get why you married him in the first place. If you married me back then and not him, we wouldn't be worrying about this today. Rushing home from vacation. Fucking Ronnie, always fucking up my plans. First he proposes to you before I do, and now this."

"Clarence, that isn't fair."

"No? I had the fucking ring, Missy."

"I know you did." She bent her head in shame.

"You're right I did. So I don't feel the least bit bad about banging my buddy's wife behind his back for almost thirty years. 'Cause you were always mine, never his."

"Clarence, I never ..."

"No, you didn't."

They held each other tight.

"I love you, baby." she said. "You're right, we shouldn't worry about him."

The Uber driver pulled up to the curb. He was thin, with a close-shaved head and glasses, who declared himself as Bob. He was a younger man, much younger than one would expect to be driving a Kia Soul and adorned in a throwback Denver Broncos John Elway jersey. After confirming the identity of his passenger, "Missy,' their luggage was loaded into the back of the small SUV. They heard

The Dark coming from the speakers of the car as it drove off.

"We'll be to our destination in roughly three hours." Bob said cheerily.

"That's great. Can you turn this shit? I hate this fucking band," Clarence told Bob.

"Sure thing!" Bob replied and The Dark became Lady Gaga.

Melissa laid her head on his shoulder, and Clarence smiled. This would all be over soon. He could finally live his life the way he wanted, with the woman he loved for the past thirty years.

"Where are you guys coming from?"

"Just drive, dude. We're not your friends." Clarence and the driver made eye contact in the rearview mirror. The driver turned his eyes down first. Clarence smiled, closed his eyes, and leaned his head back. It was a quiet ride the rest of the way to Ulster County.

CHAPTER 14

RONNIE & THE MOSIN

SUNDAY, JUNE 13, 2021, 10:30 A.M.

Ronnie's head and neck throbbed. He wondered what happened. He was lying on the cold stone tiles of his foyer. Splinters of wood, the remains of the loft's rail, covered the floor around him. He pushed himself up, burying a sliver into his right thumb. In conjunction with the hangnail on the neighboring finger, his hand throbbed worse than his head.

"Son of a bitch!" He sucked the thumb into his mouth and chewed the sliver out with his teeth. The wood ripped out and stuck him in the tongue, creating a canker sore on the tip of muscle. He spit the sliver out, again wincing in pain as his tongue was caught between his teeth. How could life be shitting on him this hard?

"This can't be happening." Ronnie resolved his luck was the worst. He pulled the rope end and saw it had snapped; the clean break looked almost as if someone cut it. His luck sucked. All of this blindsided him and came from out of nowhere. His mind started to recount the events leading up to this, yet another failed attempt to kill himself. Was it worth it? Any of it? He clenched his hand into a fist and punched the wall. Ronnie screamed so loud in pain he felt his vocal cords scratch. An uncomfortable sting of electric bolts shot up his arm. The epicenter was his hangnail ridden finger. Though covered, the wound still served as a pain magnet on his hand. His neck ached; his shoulder, which took the brunt of the fall, throbbed. But the hangnail hurt above all else, an affliction he found to be more irritating than the failed suicide attempts. Could anyone have luck as bad as Ronnie Dark's?

•

He remembered how he got to this point, the rage building within him with each passing moment. It started innocently enough. Ronnie worked on a cruise line and Melissa booked a cabin on one of his runs to spend their anniversary together. So he thought. The classic rock tribute band he played in sure rocked the boat, including a mini reunion of The Dark as drummer Beaver joined Ron and his band onstage. Ron rocked his wife's bunk soon as the set was over.

The next morning, Ronnie found himself standing before the ship's captain, charged with fraternizing with a guest. He argued he was with his wife, at which point he learned it was she who turned him in. She came forward, not to defend her husband of three decades, but to deliver him divorce papers with one hand while holding Clarence "Beaver" Allan, his former drummer and alleged best friend of the past thirty-some-odd years, with the other.

Lucky for Melissa and Beaver, ship stewards restrained Ronnie before he could throw any punches. He was thrown in the brig until they reached land. While incarcerated and as a nervous-wreck Ronnie chewed his fingernails to the quick, the cruise ship terminated his contract. Aside from his attacking a guest, which would have gotten him fired regardless, they followed a zero tolerance for fraternization with guests. When they arrived at the first U.S. Territory on their path, they left Ronnie Dark in St. Thomas.

There was enough cash on him to buy a ticket home. She, quite predictably, had drained their joint bank accounts. He'd never set up a private slush fund and now regretted it. A flight to Miami and then another to JFK, followed by a country drive north into the Catskills, and Ron found himself homeless, not a penny to his name.

Why did he bother? Nobody cared. His wife stopped caring soon as she let Clarence clean her beaver. The buck-toothed bastard's ineptness gave him a hard enough time keeping a four-four beat, but he could tie a cherry stem into a knot with his tongue and gap-teeth. Ron knew the origins of Clarence's misogynistic moniker. He got the nickname Beaver claiming it was the only meat he would eat. *How long had Melissa's beaver been on his menu?* Ron mused. *Or better yet, what has three legs and a wife stealing bastard?*

Beaver fucking Allan's drumming stool.

He wondered how much bullshit and failure he could endure. Ron knew he'd done a lot of shitty things in his life, and maybe he could have done some things better as a husband. But he never cheated on Melissa. Not once. Sure, he flirted with a lot of women. It was his job. He was a fucking rock star, for Christ's sake! But cheat? Never.

Ronnie stomped up the stairs to his bedroom. He was done fucking around. He was going to make this the last attempt. He pulled the accordion doors back, stepped into the closet, and pushed through the clothes. He brushed his infected finger against the length of the first article of clothing he moved, a long wool coat. The pain was almost welcome at this point. Ronnie didn't scream.

He smiled.

Hidden in the back behind Melissa's dresses and outfits, a long black case leaned against the wall. Ronnie grabbed it by a carrying handle midway up the length. He threw the case on his king-sized bed.

A long shelf lined the closet. On top, between plastic bins of beauty supplies and rolled linens, was a small metal container. Green, with a combination padlock on one end. A folding handle was affixed to its top.

Ronnie took this and the long, plastic case downstairs with him.

He set the metal container on the dining room table next to his dead list and suicide letter. The list stared at him.

Gun
Slit Wrists
Hanging
Pills
Carbon Monoxide
Drowning
Fire
Suffocation

He'd make this final as fuck. *Carbon Monoxide* and *Hanging* didn't work. He didn't trust the *Slit Wrists* choice or if he'd take enough *Pills* to get the job done. *Fire, Drowning,* and *Suffocation,* along with their derivatives, were out of the question by this point. This left one option. How did the wrestler Cactus Jack say it?

"Bang! Bang!" Ronnie shot invisible pistols into the air.

He dialed a combination into the lock on the metal container. The lock unclasped with a jerk. He tossed it on the table and opened the container. Inside was a stack of steel jacketed bullets, long and wicked looking with copper priming caps. Over a hundred 7.6254R rounds, long as a man's pointy finger and almost as thick as his dick. He pulled out a handful with his good hand and loaded them into a stripper clip holding half a dozen of the rounds.

Ronnie flicked up a series of clips holding the plastic case closed. It popped open as the final clip snapped up. Inside the case sat a bolt action rifle with a long barrel and a folded bayonet. The Mosin M44 carbine came from a Russian war surplus. The weapon was seventy-five years old and never touched by a dead Russian soldier. It stared back at him, the metal barrel a dull contrast to the glistening finish on the rifle's wood. He removed the rifle and loaded the stripper clip into the magazine. Ronnie held the weapon with both hands, re-familiarizing himself with the weight of the heavy rifle. It possessed an eighteen-inch retractable bayonet, and the rear butt stock was a plate of curved metal. It did nothing to cushion the weapon's recoil.

Ronnie walked into the living room and sat

back down on the sofa. He remained in silence for a few minutes before pulling the bolt back and loading a round into the chamber.

CHAPTER 15

PATRICK & SAINT D'INANA

SUNDAY, JUNE 13, 2021, 11:00 A.M.

Patrick Dermotty stood in the pump house, admiring his work in dedication to his dark goddess, Saint D'Inana. It was a glorious sight to behold. The floor was black and sticky with the blood of the sacrifices he made throughout the night before. Three gifts to his deity were required, and now he waited for a sign. It wouldn't be long, this Patrick knew. The last sacrifice would attract attention sooner than later, and he'd have to move on.

But not without Saint D'Inana. He closed his eyes, looking for a sign, some vision from his dark goddess. Something to direct him to her location. He tilted his head back and stretched his arms out from his sides, then spun about in a circle. He felt her, he was certain she was near, but where? He fell to a clump on the floor of the pump house, splashing the thin layer of gore. The hollow floor resonated with a dull thud.

He pushed up, his hands slipping in the sheen of blood covering the flooring and dropping him back down, his mask a thin shield, separating his face from the gore. It mashed his nose and lips into his skull, and he could smell Her. His goddess was here the entire time. He headbutted the floorboards, splashing blood. He did it again with the same result. A third headbutt ... and a board cracked. He jumped up to a full vertical base and stomped his right foot down on the cracked board. It snapped in the middle, revealing a void under the pump house. He reached down and pulled the floorboards up one at a time until a large portion of the flooring was removed. He opened the door, allowing the moonlight to seep in. It didn't take long for his treasure to reveal itself. Partially buried in the dirt; Patrick could see a twinkle of red.

Saint D'Inana.

He thrust his hand into the dirt and grasped the handle. He drew the short sword from the earth where it lay buried for three decades, waiting. The black blade glistened in the moon's light. Patrick's breaths became short and frantic; he was hyperventilating in expectancy. His elation froze him in place.

"Saint D'Inana," he whispered.

He held the short sword: a Roman gladius, its bronze finish stained black with a brilliant red ruby set into the base of its pommel. Strips of leather bound the blade's handle, and it lacked the traditional pommel guard often seen on a sword, giving the weapon a sleek appearance. Patrick twisted the blade in his wrist and admired its beauty. In the dirt sat a scabbard of black mahogany and leather. He reached down and grabbed it, tapping the wood and leather on a metal compressor tank. The dirt fell off.

"My Dark Lady, I am with you," he said to the blade. "What will you have me do first?" he asked and stared at the sword. A moment of silence passed before Patrick grabbed the weapon's scabbard and returned the blade to its sheath. He slid it behind his back, down his shirt and into the waist of his pants by the small of his back. The collar of his jacket held the weapon in place as Patrick Dermotty exited the shed. More sacrifices were in order. Saint D'Inana required them to grow to her full power.

CHAPTER 16

MELISSA, CLARENCE & BOB

SUNDAY, JUNE 13, 2021, 11:05 A.M.

The highway turned into county roads, twisting and turning as the ride brought him deeper into the Catskills. The speed limit would fluctuate, ranging from fifty-five down to thirty. It drove Bob Foley crazy, but not as much as his fare did. They accomplished the job without saying a goddamn word.

Bob knew when he saw this was his lady passenger's first ride, he'd have trouble. First rides were always trouble. And her name was Missy, another strike against her. He was surprised she wasn't wearing fuzzy boots and drinking pumpkin spice something out of season.

Two and a half hours of pop music was

proving him right. The club beats, thumping away, gave him a headache, but he couldn't say anything. Mr. Backseat Program Director would have a fit. He was looking at a nice payday, plus tip, from this joker and his puma girlfriend, so he dared not tempt him.

"Just drive, dude. We're not your friends." The passenger's words echoed through his memory.

Nope, you aren't my friends, Bob thought in return. If they were friends, they'd be listening to one of Bob's favorite bands from the 80s, The Dark, Manowar, or maybe The Scream, and talking about pro wrestling. But no, his riders were antisocial dicks. Bob found this to be surprising, considering he was an introvert forced into dealing with the public for this part time job. The duo sat in the back seat, silent. If not for an occasional cough or a glimpse of a brooding face in the rearview mirror, he wouldn't have thought anyone was in the car with him.

I'll be damned. If I have to be nice to you, you best be nice to me, you son of a bitch. The fare looked like a couple of rich, middle-aged former yuppies. The guy was in an obnoxious

Hawaiian short and camouflaged jams, she was in a sundress highlighting her wrinkly arms and bony armpits. Neither of them took off their sunglasses. Bob wondered why he couldn't get a famous passenger. He knew Ronnie Dark and Steve Brodie lived near Kingston, where this ride was going. Ronnie had bought the Balloon Boy Murder house, hidden somewhere in Ulster County. But no, instead he gets Mr. and Mrs. Assclown.

He gazed down at his GPS. The timer read seventeen minutes to their destination off county Route 42. A light in the backseat caught his eye, and he saw the lady was dialing a number on her phone. She set the volume up so loud, he heard the device peep as she hit the numbers on the touch screen. The line rang until the phone went straight to the other end's voicemail. The standard this-mailbox-is-full message followed without revealing the identity of the person she called. He guessed it was their pampered and spoiled adult kid who still lived at home. The woman disconnected the call and turned her screen off.

"Why do you bother?" the man said to her.

She didn't reply and Bob couldn't see her facial expression. He was almost positive it was a kid or some unreliable family member. This was the extent of conversation Bob would hear from his passengers until they arrived at their destination.

Regardless of them, it was a nice morning drive in the country, Bob resolved. The ride at least was interesting, providing the driver with plenty of mental stimulation. Earlier, while stopped at an intersection in Warwarsing, Bob watched a throng of teenage Orthodox Jews hanging out in front of a local laundromat, cleaning their clothes. Bob noted one of them, a tall boy with striking eyes and a square chin. It was clear he was the group's leader. The teen bent a crease in his black hat and left a random button on his long coat unclasped. The exhibition made Bob smile. A little bit of rebellion, hidden within the parameters of the tradition. The light changed, and soon the kids were but a memory.

As they neared the destination, Bob found his blue Kia Soul slowing to a crawl behind an Amish buggy, complete with horses and family in black and white. His car and the anachronistic buggy were a stark contrast to one another, yet oddly, they both felt in place. Much like the Orthodox Jews, it wasn't surprising for the local Amish community to be seen traveling about. He found the similarities in appearance between the two disparate groups as remarkable as their devoted faiths.

Two small children, their heads adorned in simple bonnets, peaked out of the back. As he approached, they gave him double thumbs up, which Bob returned by sticking his tongue out and making a raspberry. The kids ducked down with looks of shock on their wee faces. He slowly passed them, breaching a hill only to come upon another Amish wagon. It was mostly the same as the prior, sans the creepy children.

The Amish and their Mennonite brethren were common out here, so passing a pair of horse drawn carriages wasn't an uncommon sight. However, when he came across a third, it was becoming a bit too much. This one was a bit longer and blacker than the previous two. He wondered if he was passing by a horse drawn hearse at that point.

Holy shit, it's an Amish funeral procession, Bob thought, keeping the joke and his amusement to himself. To share the moment of mirth with Mr. Humorless in his back seat risked his tip and a bad rating. As if cued, he spoke.

"What's the hold up?"

"Some Amish, I'm almost around them. Sorry," Bob replied.

"No, you're all good. Damn fools, need to get with the times," was the last thing he said. Bob didn't bother to respond to the bigoted statement. This guy was a real gem. He was pushing Bob's buttons. Thank God the ride was almost done. For another fifteen minutes, winding down curving roads alongside rolling hills of the Catskills, they continued to ride in silence. A quarter of an hour until everything would change.

CHAPTER 17

DR. PENNOIRE & THE SHERIFFS

SUNDAY, JUNE 13, 2021, 10:35 A.M.

A command tent stood in the parking lot of the Fenton State Hospital for the Criminally Insane. Dozens of New York State Police cruisers, SUVs and vans were scattered about, intermixed with Oswego and Onondaga County Sheriff patrol cars. Policemen, troopers, and deputies milled about. Although the scene looked chaotic, there was an order to it, and it all funneled into the central command tent.

A helicopter matching the color of the State Police cruisers, blue with yellow pinstripes, flew in. A big dual engine Bell 430, it hovered over an empty parking lot adjacent to the command center before setting down. The blades chopped through the air, blowing grass and loose gravel about. No one exited the flying machine; it awaited passengers.

Across the lot at the command tent, Dr. Pennoire, flanked by her familiar bodyguards, cut a wedge through the mass of officers. The throngs parted, allowing the small contingent to move out of the structure. A State Police commander approached and intercepted the group. P. Manzene was engraved on the name badge attached to the lapel of his right breast pocket.

"Dr. Pennoire, I can't authorize a flight to Kingston. We need this bird here."

"Commander Manzene, I beg to differ. I'm certain Patrick Dermotty is in Ulster County."

"We have no evidence Dermotty is out of the area. We've put up the appropriate measures to apprehend him. There is no possible way he could have left the Central New York area. We'll catch him soon enough, up here."

"You're wrong, Commander. It wasn't done fast enough," the doctor replied.

"What makes you think he traveled nearly three hundred miles over two days by foot?"

"He didn't. I believe he stowed away on some transport from this area. A truck or a bus. This is getting us nowhere. You're only exasperating the situation. Do I need to call my friends in Washington?" Her tone was cold and direct. The commander caught his breath and returned a stern glare to the doctor.

"That's a bullshit thing to say, Pennoire. This mess is a result of the incompetence of your staff at this facility. Please, by all means, call them. Explain to them how he got away because one of your staff opened the fucking door to take him home for a date!"

"This exchange is the sort of miscommunication he's hoping we'll experience. The longer we delay, the closer he gets to his goal, if he isn't already there."

"And what goal is that? Why would he want to return to his home so badly? You'd think he'd know we'd check there first?"

"He believes the dark god he serves has a presence there."

"Isn't that nice."

"Well, is it?"

"The authorities four decades ago found nothing in a detailed scrubbing of the property during his trial. What makes you think he hid something there?"

"I know my patient." She scowled.

An unmarked squad car with Official United States Government plates pulled up next to them. The passenger's window opened. From inside the vehicle, a man in U.S. Army BDUs shouted out. It was the squad leader of the special ops team. Shiny brass captain's bars decorated his lapel. They twinkled in the morning sun.

"Incoming orders, sir, ma'am," he said, saluting the commander.

"I guess you don't have to call them, do you," Manzene said as he returned the salute. He was irritated. Pennoire ignored him, her attention instead focused on the soldier.

"Commander Manzene, Doctor Pennoire." The captain acknowledged the duo. "We received verification from the Ulster County Sheriff's Department. There was an explosion at a meth lab near the CSX train yards. Inside the remains of the lab, they found this." A photograph of a melted and twisted knife blade, the handle to which was pitted and burned. "Forensics say it's a match to the knife missing from Ms. White's apartment."

"Or a fucking train. Son of a bitch!" Dr. Pennoire said. "I knew it! I told you!" The file showed printed pictures of a disaster area. The first few were the same, aerial shots of a lingering trail of smoke, arcing into the sky. The commander had seen crime scenes like this before. Black smoke rose from behind the CSX yard in another photo. He knew a meth lab had blown. More pictures.

"According to the first responders from the train yard, the place stank of sulfur and horseradish, and a yellow fog hung about the place. He said he tied a bandanna around his mouth and nose and pulled his train goggles down over his eyes. He took this picture on his phone."

It was a body. At least it was a human, once. The commander wasn't sure if it belonged to a man or a woman, but the safe odds were on it being male. He couldn't tell from the clothing. The skin and flesh had dripped off the appendages at some point, leaving skeletal arms and useless hands.

The victim laid on the ground, their face blistered and burned beyond recognition. Blood and fluid dripped from the lips and nose, and there was no doubt the person was dead. They weren't alone. On the corpse's lap was something odd. Between the hands, the exposed flesh around the fingers blistered and dripping pus and blood, was an anomaly.

"My God," Manzene thought, but said aloud. It was a mistake to speak. The pictures were so real and fresh, his mind tricked him. He tasted the chemicals and the thought made his tongue tingle. The odor's familiarity hovered somewhere in the neighborhood of rancid dog shit, bleach, and sulfur. It all made him feel uncomfortable as if his own flesh was exposed to the chemical agents.

"One of their sheriff deputies, Sergeant Jolene Stevens, has gone missing. Her last known whereabouts were in the vicinity of the Dick residence, late last night. The department was going to send another car out to the location. I prevented that."

"Well done, Captain," Pennoire commended him.

"They are on stand-by, putting together a S.W.A.T. team and awaiting your arrival."

"Very good."

"Also, it's worth mentioning, no one has been able to reach Mr. Dick's associate, Steve

Brudzinski, aka Steve Brodie, for two days. According to Mrs. Dark, she directed him to go to the property on Friday night."

Dr. Pennoire looked Commander Manzene in the eye.

"Well, Phil?" Her ice blue eyes didn't blink. His did.

"Go, Amanda. And find out how he fucking got there. You should be back on the ground in ... I don't know, ninety minutes? Shorter if the wind is with you."

"Oh, it will be," Dr. Pennoire replied, and along with her bodyguards, the trio made haste across the tarmac to the waiting chopper.

CHAPTER 18

RONNIE & THE MOSIN

SUNDAY, JUNE 13, 2021, 11:05 A.M.

Ronnie Dark sat on the sofa in his living room with his M44 Mosin draped across his lap. From the sofa, he was treated to a nice view of the valley next to his house out the bay windows. And he could see his reflection, a phantasm in the tall panes of glass. Motionless, he stared, a blank expression on his face, at the forest beyond his translucent image.

He grasped the weapon by the barrel and placed the stock on the floor, between his legs. The tip of the barrel was just above the top of his head as he sat on the couch. The damn carbine was long, about forty inches, and to get the right angle he'd have to lean the rifle out. He realized right away pulling the trigger was going to be problematic.

Why can't a fucking thing be easy for me? He tried putting the barrel under his chin. He couldn't reach the trigger. He put it on his forehead, could slip his finger in the trigger guard, but the barrel would slip off. He was coming to the conclusion this wasn't going to work either. He tried to think of something he could procure, a device or implement he could use to pull the trigger without jeopardizing the desired outcome. He thought about getting a coat hanger, bending it to suit his needs. Then he remembered all the coat hangers in the house were plastic.

All there was left to do was squeeze the trigger. He racked his brains, trying to come up with a plan. Then it came to him: the pen he'd been writing with all weekend would suffice. He set the rifle against the sofa cushion, stood up, walked to the table, and took the pen and inspected it. It looked to be long enough. Satisfied it would do the job, Ronnie placed it behind his ear and returned to the sofa. The rifle slid off the leather covered cushion when Ronnie sat down, clanging onto the tile floor. He bent over to pick it up and grazed his bad finger on the rifle.

"Son of a bitch!" he swore. Once again life was shitting on Ronnie as much as it could before he could end his miserable existence. Pain from the hangnail arced throughout his hand. He grabbed the rifle with his left hand, pulled the bolt back to ensure a round was in the chamber. It was. He stuck it between his knees, stock on the floor. The metal scraped on the stone tile, leaving a long, white scratch in the flooring.

Oh fucking well, Ronnie thought as he looked down and saw it. He turned it into an X with another scrape, then smiled. He'd left one more mark to remember him by. The X to mark the spot he died in. He held the stock with his feet and placed the barrel under his chin. He could smell the gun oil, its neutral, metallic scent tickled his nostrils. Ronnie pinched the pen in his right hand, between his thumb, middle, and ring fingers, being careful not to use his infected forefinger. He turned his eyes down, straining them in his head, to watch the pen and guide it to the trigger.

His infected finger brushed a clamp on the rifle's forward grip and snagged the fraying Band-aid. Agonizing bolts of electric pain numbed his hand and wrist. He dropped the pen. It bounced next to his foot on the tile. He moved his foot and kicked the pen across the floor, toward the windows, a few feet away.

"Motherfucker! Of course this happens! God fucking damn it all to Hell!" He would need to retrieve the pen. Nothing was easy. Not one fucking thing. Ronnie moved the rifle aside and stood up.

He felt something tickle the air behind him, starting by his neck and continuing down in a straight line, parallel to his spine. An explosion of air released as fabric was ripped. A feeling of dread replaced the sensation of pain from his finger. A flash of red caught his eye. The guitarist's attention turned from the pen on the floor to the bay windows.

What the fuck? Before Ronnie Dark, in the window, was his own semi-transparent reflection. And standing behind his reflection was a tall man in dark overalls and a wrestler's mask. The white and black pattern on the mask resembled a dragon's skull. The shape raised its arms up. Ronnie saw the would-be assailant was armed.

With a short, red and black sword.

"Would you like to buy a vowel?" The shape declared, his voice sounding so polite and professional.

He sounds just like a fucking gameshow host, Ronnie thought as the shape raised the sword over his head and swung it at the guitarist's neck.

CHAPTER 19

RONNIE, PATRICK & SAINT D'INANA

SUNDAY, JUNE 13, 2021, 11:15 A.M.

"You're the next contestant on The Sacrifice is Right!" the masked man said, still hamming it up with the game show announcer voice. The sword bit into the back of the sofa a second time. Ronnie spun around and faced the invader. His heart pounded in his chest. The masked man didn't speak further. Ron didn't necessarily give him enough time to say anything. The guitarist fumbled with the rifle, raised it to his shoulder, and pointed the barrel. His bandaged finger found the trigger. The pain from the pressure on the hangnail was excruciating.

"Who the fuck are you?" Ronnie exclaimed as he squeezed. Fuck giving this guy a chance to respond.

The Mosin erupted, spitting a ball of flame

a yard out of the gun's muzzle. Ronnie's ears were dulled. He forgot how loud the M44 was. It was a portable cannon, and in the confined space of the house, the report was deafening. The .30 caliber projectile spun down the length of the grooved barrel at twenty-six hundred feet per second. The guitarist and the masked man were thrown to the floor in unison by the weapon's recoil. Both men grunted in pain. The rifle fell beside Ron on the tiles. He heard the invader's sword clatter as it skipped across the floor.

Did I hit him? Holy shit, did I shoot a man? The words ran through Ronnie's mind at lightning speed. Did it matter? He resolved in an instant. *The guy just tried to cut your head off with a fucking sword! Who the fuck is this joker?* Ronnie stood, retrieving the rifle as he did. He pulled the bolt back and ejected the smoking, spent shell of the 7.6254R round. It bounced off his wrist and landed on the floor, rattling about with a sharp din.

"Don't make me shoot you again, motherfucker!" he said as he pointed the carbine at nothing. He hit his infected finger on the trigger guard again, but the adrenaline running through his body dulled the pain to nothing. He tried to find something to aim at. There was nothing.

The sofa obscured the intruder, this much was certain. Ronnie didn't know if he lived or was missing a substantial portion of his upper body. The guitarist knew the damage his rifle could do. He'd seen it blow out the back of a large pumpkin: one little hole in the front with nothing left in the back. He looked down, seeking the pool of blood one would find with such a wound. There was none. A pair of booted feet laid prone, exposed from the edge of the piece of furniture.

"Fuck this!" Ronnie declared. He stood his ground, sweeping the barrel of the rifle to his left and right, alert for the intruder to stand. Ron backed up, deliberate and slow, making his way to the dining room, away from the parlor, keeping his eyes on the sofa. And the intruder's feet. He brought the rifle's stock up to his shoulder, aimed down, and made his way around the sofa. First he saw the sword, far enough away from the body for it to be a non-factor. Then he saw the sword wielder, lying on the floor.

"Fuck you, motherfucker!" The guitarist pointed the rifle at the intruder's head. But he didn't pull the trigger. Part of him wanted to know who this guy was and why he picked Ronnie fucking Dark to shish-kabob. He stood, aiming the rifle at the man for a few more moments until he was sure the guy wasn't getting up. Or as certain as he could be. His mind went back to dozens of horror movies he watched over the years. *Halloween, Friday the 13th*, Freddy. All of them shared one thing in common. It was the end of numerous police officers, boyfriends, and girlfriends. The motherfucking killer got back up after you shot him.

If I shot him. Ronnie corrected his inner monologue. Still, curiosity was getting the best of him. He needed to know what this asshole looked like. He crept around the still body, pointing the gun down at it the entire time. He wasn't taking any chances. If the guy moved, Ronnie was blasting him. He knelt at the intruder's mask covered head, took his hand off the trigger, and yanked the mask off.

It took Ronnie a moment to figure out who the blood covered face belonged to. A dirty growth of a graying beard covered most of it. But under all of that, Ronnie saw his eyes, those deep crazy eyes. And Ronnie knew who this was.

Patrick Dermotty.

"Son of a bitch." Ronnie said, standing up. He looked at the mask grasped in his fist. The fabric brushed against his hangnail, causing his arm to twitch. He leaned the rifle against the wall. And put the mask on. The room went gray through the knitted eye slits. Ronnie felt off, then the vertigo hit him.

•

Ronnie wasn't in the room anymore. He was outside and a blazing sun was burning down on him. Sand and dust were everywhere, as far as he could see from under the mask. It felt heavy on his head, like it was more than a mask now. He reached up with a hand. He banged his finger off metal, mesh, and fabric.

Why doesn't that hurt? he thought. The hangnail he'd fought all day ... was gone?

He looked at his hand. It wasn't Ronnie's

hand. He looked at the other. He grasped a charcoal black short sword; Ron recognized it as a Roman gladius. But it wasn't Ronnie's hand gripping the wicked looking blade with a red gemstone shining in the base of its pommel.

Is this a virtual reality thing? he wondered. Did the mask have some technology in it? The guitarist pondered on this for a moment. Until the ground shook and Ronnie no longer cared. He looked forward. A blurred shape grew from a speck to an ominous cloud of terror. He heard a roar increase in resonance. A pair of red dots broke through the fog. They stared into Ronnie Dark. He felt his mind being violated by something. A vile, sick something. He could feel its desires, its wants, its needs, and it wanted Ronnie.

"No, no, no, no!" Ronnie screamed aloud. He slammed his hand, Ronnie's real hand, onto the sword, knowing where the hangnail was. The pain came to life on impact. It shot up his arm and into his brain, breaking him out of the vision. The dust swirled and dissipated, but the room was spinning at a high-G velocity.

And Ronnie blacked out...

... for only a second...

...but a second is an eternity in the cosmos...

·

● ● ● **A**nd then he was falling, spinning away, hands over feet through a vortex. Rainbows of Aurora Borealis swirled about his tumbling body. Celestial bodies streaked around his peripheral, mixed with a canopy of stars racing past him. Ronnie felt like he dropped into a Sid Barrett era Pink Floyd song. All he needed to do now was set the controls for ... somewhere else.

Everything stopped. Ronnie was standing in a house, but not his house. It was another time, not too long ago, but long enough to be different. A console TV set graced the living room; a rotary dial telephone hung on the wall. The clock next to it was analog. Carpeting the color of goldenrod graced the floors.

Up to the pool of blood encircling the bodies in the living room.

A large, muscular man, naked, except for a black and white wrestling mask—the same mask Ronnie wore—stood over them, brandishing an all too familiar black short sword. Ronnie noted the man was hung like a Greek hero.

Instead of staring at the naked man's miniscule manhood, Ronnie focused his vision on the bodies: a blonde woman and a young boy with black hair. Both were smiling and staring at Ronnie with dead, white eyes. They were hogtied, their hands and legs bound together behind their backs, lying on their bellies. Their throats were cut open, giving each the appearance of a second mouth.

"For Saint D'Inana!" the naked man croaked out. The words were followed with a hideous and raspy laugh. He held the sword before himself, between the woman and child.

And fell upon the blade, driving it into his chest.

The room spun again, blurring in motion, setting Ronnie off balance.

"Fuck this!" he shouted, and threw himself to the floor.

•

"**W**hat the fuck did I just see?" a nauseated Ronnie exclaimed. He pulled the mask up over his eyes and saw he was prone on the floor, next to the Balloon Boy. Closing his eyes and shaking his head, he tried to get the visions to leave. It didn't work. The memory of what he saw remained burned into his psyche. He didn't want to be anywhere near this guy. He looked straight ahead and saw the door to the garage was open. The mask slipped back down, catching on the bridge of his nose.

Time to jet, he thought, and Ronnie got up and hopped down the stairs.

He slammed the door behind him, but it bounced back open, repelled by the remaining duct tape sticking to the door and frame. The door slammed against the wall, giving Ron a moment to pause. He looked over his shoulder and was relieved to see no one followed. He traversed the garage, passing the disabled Corvette and avoiding the debris littering the floor, moving to the side door. He exited the building and stepped outside. Still, no one pursued him. Maybe the masked man was dead, but Ronnie highly doubted it.

The shadow of the house fell on the lawn and driveway. Ron could see bits of the sun poking through the canopy of trees surrounding the property. The full parking lot caught his attention. In the lot, he saw an Ulster County Sheriff's patrol car sitting next to a familiar red SUV. Brodie's Jeep.

Why would Brodie and the cops be here? he thought.

"Help! Help me! Someone is trying to kill me!" he screamed, not knowing what else to do. No one answered his pleas. Ronnie looked up and saw a black shape inside the house, hovering in front of the bay windows. Ron knew the motherfucker was watching him. Who the hell was he, anyhow?

Ron ran up to the patrol car, the Mosin in one hand. The car was empty; it looked as if someone had run the front panel instruments through a blender. Brodie's Jeep suffered the same fate.

Ronnie looked back up to the windows. The shape was gone. This unsettled him. The lunatic could show up anywhere now. He noticed his suitcases on the porch and wondered how and when they got there. He turned and twisted his head, his eyes frantic as they scanned the area, looking for any sign of a random sheriff's deputy or his friend ...

... or the guy with a sword.

"Brodie? Steve?" No one answered. The guitarist ran to the back yard. Maybe someone—anyone—was there.

Ronnie Dark was about to discover how right he was.

The musician dashed to the back yard, looking for whoever might be back there. The morning sun shone through the tree line, casting a spotlight on the semi-enclosure. It was empty except for the shed, pool, and pump house. The doors to the shed were still open, but no people milled about the back. No Steve, no police officer.

He ran to the shed and looked in. Nobody was in it. Ron was surprised at how much he could see through the eyelets of the mask he wore. No wonder Brodie didn't mind wearing one when they sang the Balloon Boy's song. The thought of the killer gave him pause. Paranoid, the masked guitarist looked back behind him to the house. He shook in terror, afraid he might see the fucking Balloon Boy standing there with a shit eating grin on his blood-soaked face, complete with a blow-up sausage dog. He wasn't, much to Ron's relief.

Ronnie could see the pump house doors were ajar. He exited the shed, and a half dozen steps later, Ron stood before the doors.

Something didn't smell right. It was a fetid, nauseating stench, reminiscent of a cat box left shit and piss ridden for two weeks. It lingered through the chlorine and chemical smell the shed normally emitted and made Ron's eyes water twice as badly.

"What fucking died in here?" he said, pulling the mask down, hoping it would shield him from the odor, and opened the door. Ronnie dropped the Mosin. It crashed into the flooring with a loud crack. He immediately regretted three things:

Opening the doors, his choice of words, and pulling the mask back down.

CHAPTER 20

MELISSA, CLARENCE & BOB

SUNDAY, JUNE 13, 2021, 11:20 A.M.

"Turn left and your destination will be on the left … You've arrived." the GPS AI's voice trumpeted over the car's speakers as Bob Foley pulled up to the trip's destination. It was a private road and driveway. Bob sighed in exasperation. This confirmed his passengers were rich pricks with a house hidden away off the main road. He wished he could drop them off on the curb, but Lord knew how long this driveway was. He slowed the Soul down and turned onto the drive.

He drove slowly, following the twists and turns of the private drive. And just about a half mile later, the mansion these twats lived in came into view. It was huge, two stories high and spread out over twenty-seven hundred square feet. The property was surrounded by a near impenetrable forest. It was the perfect hidden palace.

And Bob hated them even more for owning it.

The driveway in front of a two-bay attached garage was almost filled with a Jeep and an Ulster County Sheriff's patrol car. This gave Bob the assumption Mr. Hawaiian Shirt was a cop. Bob assumed he must be crooked too.

Ain't no way a man on a deputy's salary could afford a place like this, he thought as he pulled the Kia into the one empty spot, next to a Jeep. He dropped the car into park and hopped out to help them with their bags. He saw a pair of suitcases on the porch of the house, which he found a little odd.

Did they have bags shipped home too? he wondered as he made his way to the back of the Kia. He opened the trunk, the blue gate moving up slow and sure on hydraulic hinges.

"I got them, don't worry about it," Officer Hawaiian Shirt said, stepping in between Bob and the open hatch.

"Whatever, man, your call. Just close the trunk, would you, please?" Bob turned and walked away. He was in no mood to argue with a dick who might call his friends in the sheriff's department and have them harass him on his way out. The guy grunted something Bob couldn't make out. The driver went back to his driver's seat, buckled himself back in, and waited for the trunk to close.

It took forever. The lady didn't touch one of the bags. Not a single one. She made the man unload all of them, unstuffing the Kia's trunk and piling the luggage onto the driveway. Minutes later, when the chore ended, Bob waited to ensure the people and their bags were a safe distance away, he backed out, turned the car around, and drove off.

"Good fucking riddance!" Bob proclaimed. He ended the ride on his phone app and turned on his radio, full blast.

"Drink the Kool-Aid!" Steve Brodie shouted out of the speakers. Bob noticed the Uber app acted a little funny, as if it was a delayed reaction to his command. He stopped the car, out of sight of the house and the passengers. The driver waited a few more minutes until the ride completed. It didn't show his fare, and when Bob noted the single bar on his LTE, he knew the app was fucked. So Bob and his Kia Soul drove away from the mansion in search of a better tower signal.

·

Melissa waited for Clarence to drag their luggage onto the porch before she knocked on the door. It took him forever. His shirt was soaked with perspiration and he looked miserable. She didn't care. She liked being waited on, and neither Ron nor Beaver ever questioned it. She told Beaver to pile the baggage up next to Ronnie's. She wondered why Ron had left his luggage outside. Was he even here? She knocked and rang the doorbell. No one came to the door.

"Don't you have a key?" Beaver asked, wiping beads of sweat off his brow.

"Well, yeah, but what if he's naked or has company?"

"Like you haven't seen him nude before? You were married thirty years, for fuck's sake. I don't get you sometimes, blondie."

"Fuck you, Clarence. Let me call him." She

reached into her purse to retrieve her phone. It wasn't there. She opened the bag up and peered inside. No phone. She pulled out the house keys and held them in her free hand. "Are you kidding me?"

"What?"

"I left my phone in the Uber."

"You what?"

"You heard me. Son of a bitch!"

"Are you sure you didn't drop it somewhere over here?"

"I don't know. Call it, would you? We're fucked if I left it in the Uber. I used my app to book the ride."

"Chill, already," Beaver told Melissa and dialed the phone. It rang and rang and rang and they didn't hear the ring tone, at least within ear shot.

"Shit, it's in that guy's car."

"So, what do we do?"

"I don't know. Maybe use the app on your phone to contact them?" She put the key in the door. "Let's go inside and take care of it." She turned the tumbler.

"Okay, let me load it up." Beaver stood behind Melissa; his face was buried in his phone, opening the app. Melissa turned the knob and opened the door.

"Ronnie, are you here?" she shouted. The house was dark, the only light coming from the open window. She turned her head to see where her boyfriend was. "Come on, Beave," she commanded, and stepped into her house on instinct, before turning her head back.

The odds are slight, but Melissa Dark might have gotten away if she was paying attention to her surroundings. If she saw the ruined railing to the loft, the pieces of wood and rope on the floor, perhaps she wouldn't have entered the home. She heard someone scream her name from inside the house.

"Melissa, no!" It caught her unaware and made her jump in place.

Ronnie? She thought, then turned her head to it. Someone not Ronnie answered.

"You are the weakest link, goodbye!"

Melissa Dark screamed in the final moments of her life.

•

Bob was five miles away from his last ride when he heard his favorite song from The Dark, an obscure little ditty called "United We Stand" off the band's first album, *Room*. It wasn't emanating from his car's speakers. It was coming from the back seat.

What the hell? he thought. He looked in the back seat and saw the soft glow of a cell phone lighting up. *The dumb bitch left her phone in my car? Is this for fucking real?* Bob resolved it was Murphy's Law. When one thing went south with a customer, everything went south, a giant shit snowball rolling downhill, ready to splat on Bob's Uber rating. Bob was an atheist, but it didn't stop him from contemplating which deity he pissed off to deserve this bullshit. He was cursed to deal with these motherfuckers until he died, of this he was certain.

He couldn't reach the phone in the back seat; it was out of his reach. Bob resolved to pull over as soon as he could. If he knew one thing about passengers and their cell phones, they want them right back.

It wasn't long before Bob found an

abandoned gas station on the roadside, its windows boarded over and the pumps removed out front. There was trash and overgrowth, but the parking lot was otherwise free of debris.

Bob leaned his seat back, blindly reached behind his head, and grabbed hold of the phone. He sat back up and saw the missed call icon. 'Beaver' it declared.

"Beaver?" Bob said aloud as he thought it. He swiped the phone and it opened. And there it was, on the phone's screensaver, a picture of the woman, Ronnie Dark, Steve Brodie, Lightning, and Beaver Allan. He knew he saw the guy someplace before! Beaver was the asshole in the Hawaiian shirt. Bob didn't recognize him as an overweight, middle aged man. The Beaver Bob knew possessed long blonde locks and held an athletic physique from playing the drums. Sometime during his life, much to Bob's dismay, his hero drummer had turned into a Ron Pearlman clone in a flowery shirt and jams. This meant the woman was one person: Melissa Dark, Ronnie's wife!

He stared at the picture, not believing what was so true. They say never meet your heroes;

they'll always disappoint you. The statement couldn't be truer. The house, it must be the Dark mansion. Bob shook his head in disbelief.

The phone rang, startling him. It was Beaver calling again. *What did he want?* Bob wondered, then answered the call, and the phone's video screen brought horror to life in a manner Bob's nightmares never dreamed possible ...

CHAPTER 21

RONNIE & THE DEAD

CHAPTER 21

RONNIE & THE DEAD

SUNDAY, JUNE 13, 2021, 11:20 A.M.

Ronnie heaved, causing an involuntary expulsion of the limited contents in his stomach. It all caught in the mask, covering his mouth, squishing out and around it. Some of it went up his nose. He ripped the bottom of the mask off his chin, exposing his mouth and allowing free passage for the vomit. Digestive acid burned his sinuses and throat as bile and mucus trailed out of his mouth. It created glistening, spider-web-like strands stretching to the ground at his feet. The viscous, semi-clear liquid pooled and spread, seeping under the rifle's barrel.

Steve Brodie, Ronnie Dark's one-time best friend sat before him; his eyes, once vibrant and blue, were now glazed and lifeless. His mouth hung agape, the thick curly beard crushed into his chest. His face was pale, as if he lived half the year in the part of Alaska where it stays dark all day. Brodie's hands held a balloon Santa Claus's head. It was probably a recreation of Brodie, after all; with the beard, he did resemble Santa, some. His midsection was cut open. Crimson streaks covered his lap, ending in a pile of shit-filled guts draping onto the floor out of the gaping wound.

•

The mask bound Ronnie to Patrick, creating more than a symbolic link. Through the mask's eye slits, Ronnie could see how it all went down ... first from Patrick's point of view, then from the victims', one by one. Each a sacrifice to the Balloon Boy's dark god.

No. Not a god.

His goddess.

Saint D'Inana.

Now Ronnie saw it all as it transpired ...

•

Steve woke up when the Balloon Boy threw him on top of the cabinet in the pump house. He could smell the chemicals stored beneath him; they were eye watering. He wobbled, seeking balance, leaning forward. A hand and arm, firm and solid as a steel pipe, pushed him back, slamming his back against the wall of the pumphouse.

The first slice across his midsection with the short Gladiator sword released the contents restrained behind Brodie's abdominal muscles. It didn't hurt as much as he felt relief, much like after you let out a massive fart or unbutton your pants after a Thanksgiving feast. Liquid warmth covered his legs, soaking through his jeans. He heard the dripping of something viscous on the floorboards.

A tight pull, followed by another, sent a bullet of pain coursing through his body's core, a cramping, gut twisting pang. And another. And another. And with each twist, Brodie found himself falling further and further away from the light and into the darkness. He forced his eyes open, took as big a breath as he could, pulling the air in with his chest muscles, considering his diaphragm was useless.

The Balloon Boy was busy tying off the last bit of his offering through Brodie ...

•

Next to Steve, a dead man Ronnie didn't recognize with short blonde hair sat. His head was split open, and a little bit of the skull was missing near the right temple, exposing a bit of gray matter. The corpse listed to the left, leaning against Brodie's shoulder to stay upright. His arms and face were covered in blood and tattoos. He held a balloon guitar in his hands, the faux cord attached to an amplifier somewhere deep within the guy's bowels. Across the knuckles of the man's left hand, from thumb to pinky, was the word *Mason*, and Ronnie knew how his luggage found its way to the porch...

•

Mason felt his head bounce against every possible thing it could from the accident site to wherever the fuck this guy was dragging him. Tree limbs, stumps, rocks, and concrete curbs made for his bludgeoning. He didn't feel good. Hanging upside down in a driver's seat for Lord knows how long, and now this? He was sure he was concussed. He wanted to throw up, and it got worse when they reached what turned out to be their destination. The stench of shit, piss, and drying blood greeted Mason's sense of smell, then his assailant stopped dragging him, picked his limp, semi-conscious form up, and leaned him against another person.

He could tell the other guy was dead, about as dead as Mason was going to be, he was certain of this. The assumptions were soon put to rest. Mason detected a stinging sensation near his already bruised and battered stomach. Then the air came out of his mouth and his eviscerated abdomen. The last thing Mason Pilot heard was a soft, gentle farting sound as the air escaped from his lungs out through the wound...

•

And then there was the missing sheriff, a lady deputy no less. A pair of mirrored aviator sunglasses covered her eyes. She was pretty, and Ronnie wished they had met under better, and less dead, circumstances. He could make out the name on the badge. It read *Stevens*. She held a bouquet of red, pink, and white balloon roses in her blood-soaked hands. The long stems grew from deep within her bisected abdomen ...

•

Jolene wondered what she did to deserve such a fate. One shitty, absent-minded mistake. One fucking mistake in her decades long career. But, she resolved, one mistake was all it took to get you killed. The perp—she was sure it was a mature and thirty-five years older Patrick Dermotty—dragged her by the hair from the house to the backyard. She clawed at his hands with her fingers, digging her nails into the flesh of his hands. He didn't release the hold. Her head throbbed in white lances of pain from her scalp as he yanked her hundred-and-twenty-pound frame from the house, through the garage, and to the backyard of the property.

He whipped her up into the air by the neck, and she heard a soft crack, almost like hard plastic snapping. Her body below her neck went numb in unison with the snap. Jolene watched, helpless, as Patrick Dermotty proceeded to disembowel her and craft something out of her small intestine. She saw it was a flower. The flower was the last thing she saw before the blood drained from her brain, shutting it and the consciousness once known as Jolene Stevens down...

•

Ronnie couldn't bear to look at the scene of carnage, the altar to the Balloon Boy's evil, twisted deity any longer. He picked up the rifle, made sure a shell was in the chamber. There was. Ron pulled the bayonet up out of its housing and slid it over the barrel's tip. It turned the rifle into a formidable polearm, giving Ronnie a huge advantage over a person armed with a short sword. He took one last look at his dead friend and the other two victims. He made the sign of the cross, closed the door, and ran back to the garage. It was time to end this bullshit.

Raising the rifle before entering, making sure to clear the area before moving into the house. If the son of a bitch was still lying on the floor of the living room, Ronnie was going to put a 7.6254R bullet into the motherfucker's skull, like he should have done before. Slow and sure, Ronnie made his way through the garage to the house.

The doorbell rang.

Who could be here? Ronnie thought. *More cops*? He hoped so. He waited a moment to see if he heard anything else. There was nothing. He moved as silent as he could, tiptoeing into the house. He reached the dining room, then the living room. Across the way was the front door. He heard a rattling at the knob. Someone was inserting a key.

It has to be Melissa, Ronnie thought. The door opened, and bright, white light shone in, obscuring who opened it. Then he saw the light covered by a thick, dark shadow holding a sword at arm's length. It was Patrick.

"*Melissa, no!*" Ronnie shouted and ran into the room, charging Patrick with the rifle, the bayonet cutting a path through the air between them ...

CHAPTER 22

PATRICK, MELISSA, CLARENCE & BOB

SUNDAY, JUNE 13, 2021, 11:29 A.M.

Melissa heard the scream of her ex-husband, the reply of a stranger impersonating a gameshow host. She turned her head toward the sounds and moved, walking through the threshold of the house. She knew the layout of the home and could navigate it with her eyes closed. This wasn't any different.

Until she walked into the exposed blade of a razor-sharp gladius. On first contact, along with seeing Ronnie, Melissa let out a banshee wail. The sword, however, pierced her skin between her ribs and slid through the bone and organs with ease. Melissa's left lung was deflated from the insertion, and she found, as her cry turned into a garble, she couldn't scream anymore.

Clarence, bent over and too busy fucking

around with his phone, followed her. When she stopped in front of him, he bumped her forward with his head, pushing the blade through her body. There was about a microsecond left for him to wonder what caused the sharp headache, when on reflex he jerked his head up. The sword's near monofilament blade, having pierced his skull, carved down his face through bone and flesh in an arc. Beaver's right eye and cheek, along with a chunk of his tongue, slid down and plopped on the porch deck with a wet slap.

The massive leak in Melissa's vascular system squirted blood out holes in her chest and back. She twitched, shivered, and her arms fell limp at her sides. Moving caused a sharp pain in her chest unlike any she ever felt before.

"No! You bastard!" Ronnie Dark screamed, a visage of dementia and madness.

Melissa's ex-husband burst out of the darkness behind the guy with the sword. He ran across the living room with a rifle in his hands, screaming an angry battle cry as he did. Her eyes grew wide with hope. She wondered why he wore a black and white mask. It was pulled up over his mouth and nose. In the end it didn't matter. What mattered was he came for her.

Ronnie! Her white knight, coming to her rescue. Yes, he was a shithead and lousy at giving Melissa the sexual attention she craved. But she could never deny his empathy or his compassion for her. Then all the optimism she built after seeing him drained out of her like blood from an open wound. Her murderer threw a haymaker with his free hand, catching Ronnie square in the jaw and sending him tumbling to the floor. The rifle flew from Ron's hands, sticking into the floor by its long bayonet, fluttering like a giant switchblade knife.

Melissa took as big a breath as her collapsed lung would allow her to. Excruciating pain surged through her whole being, and in the moment, Melissa regretted all she put Ronnie through. But she knew it didn't matter. Much like her secret lover of three decades, Melissa Dark was pretty goddamned dead by the time she released her last breath and her impaled body stopped twitching.

Patrick withdrew the sword, grinning, drool and saliva dripping from his lips. Both bodies fell to the floor with unceremonious thuds.

•

Bob Foley held Melissa Dark's cellphone in his hand. His eyes were glued to the screen, locked in without expression. He wasn't sure what he was watching. Was it a low budget indie splatter movie? Or some European art house horror affair, like a Serbian Film? Was it a snuff film? Or better yet, why would someone want to send her this sick fucking shit?

He tried processing what he saw from the beginning. Bob knew Ronnie was a horror fan. Many of The Dark's songs were horror related. But this?

The other phone's camera was focused on a scene of carnage. Blood, in varying shades of crimson and black, covered everything. A balding, middle-aged man stood before two prone bodies lying in pools of viscera. In his left hand he held a Gladiator sword. The red gems in the sword's black handle twinkled in the sunlight. He stabbed the sword into the flooring next to one of the bodies.

The man then reached into one of the bodies. Bob blinked and shook his head. Did he see it right? Bob focused on the video screen. The guy's arms were elbow deep in the body. The hands pulled out, revealing a knot of intestines in his grasp. Blood splattered and splashed about. The offal resembled raw sausage links in pink casing. The man rose a length of the entrails to eye level. At first, Bob thought he was going to eat it.

But he didn't. Instead, he sliced the viscera into two long pieces.

The chef? Butcher? Bob didn't know what to call this guy, extending and stretching the remaining length, like a balloon getting prepped to be turned into something resembling not a balloon. He brought it to his lips, yes, but not to eat it, oh no. He pinched one end and blew into it. Fecal matter mixed with gore ejected from the opposite end. The guy smiled. His lips were smeared with shit and blood. He smiled right at the phone, and the call ended.

Bob could feel the bile rising up his esophagus. He was terrified, knowing he had just watched the infamous Balloon Boy Killer in action, fresh out of the nut ward. This couldn't be good. He tossed the phone on the seat, no longer wanting to touch it. He wiped his hand off on his pant leg. A look of disgust covered his face, as if he ate something bad or sank his fingers knuckle deep in baby shit.

The phone sat on the seat for a few more miles until Bob could pull his Kia Soul over onto the side of the highway. He took the cell phone and wiped it down with a cloth. Satisfied with his work, Bob rolled the passenger's window down and threw Melissa Dark's phone out the window. It skipped down an embankment before splashing into the river below. Bob wanted nothing more to do with this crazy ass bullshit. He sat still and quiet for a few minutes before deciding to leave. The Uber driver put the Soul into drive.

Foley thought he heard the sirens first, lending him to pause and look both ways an extra time or two. He then saw the lights in his peripheral vision before he let his foot off the brake. One, then two, and finally a third Ulster

County Sheriff patrol car sped by with their lights working overtime. Bob wondered where they might be going, then disregarded the thought as he pressed the accelerator. Bob Foley drove away, wishing to distance himself as far as he could from Melissa Dark's cell phone.

CHAPTER 23

RONNIE, PATRICK & DR. PENNOIRE

SUNDAY, JUNE 13, 2021, 11:40 A.M.

D r. Amanda Pennoire and her bodyguards sat in the sheriff's patrol car, not saying a word from the moment they got into the vehicle in Kingston. The location of the house was isolated. Amanda thought of having the helicopter take them to the property, but the forest and terrain prevented it. The drive from Kingston to the Dark house would take almost another hour. Amanda wasn't sure if anyone at the property would have an hour if Patrick was there. If it was still there.

This was forty-five minutes ago.

Now a trio of patrol cars, sirens blazing, sped down the county highways, hugging the curves at maximum velocity.

•

"Melissa!" Ronnie screamed as the black shape stepped out from the shadows, obscuring anything near the front door of the house. He ran and leapt into the air, the rifle held over his head like a polearm. He was ready to strike Dermotty and put an end to this madness. He didn't count on meeting Patrick's ham-fist. The blow caught Ron in the sternum, a sledgehammer strike knocking the wind out of the guitarist.

Ronnie tumbled across the floor, his arms and legs splayed, his head hollow and resonating from the impact. He watched, dumbfounded, as Patrick withdrew the Gladiator sword from his ex-wife. He gaped in horror as her body fell to the floor. It ended up becoming a bittersweet moment. Part of him was sad about Melissa; he supposed that couldn't be avoided. But Ron wasn't surprised one bit at the elation he felt when he saw Beaver also got the shish kabob treatment, with a side of face carving thrown in for good measure.

Fucker. Wife stealing prick. Good riddance,

he thought, momentarily worried he said it out loud. After all, he didn't want to disrespect the dead, at least not so anyone, especially his murderer, could hear. He gathered his wits and stood. His rifle was stuck in the tile floor, blade first. He doubted he could reach it before the fucking Balloon Boy could cut him in half with the fucking sword. Besides, what could he do if he got the rifle? Duel the motherfucker?

Eddie Van Halen vs. Freddy. *Why did that never happen?* Ron thought to himself. It would have been a sure money maker back in the day!

Patrick turned to face Ronnie, the lunatic's eyes burning with hatred and anger. Ron looked for something, anything to fight the serial killer with. There wasn't a damn thing, no fireplace pokers, no walking sticks, none of the traditional items you would find in a slasher movie. And why was it this way? Because this wasn't a movie. It was real life. And real life always seemed to enjoy fucking Ronnie Dark in the ass without spitting.

What he saw was a clean exit back through the garage and away from this guy. He didn't hesitate; he knew there was no room for error. This motherfucker was going to kill him and make balloon animals out of his guts. Ronnie ran as fast as his legs would allow, through the living room, dining room, and into the garage. He leaped, skipping the four steps leading down into the garage.

•

Patrick didn't follow Ronnie, oh no. Patrick would find him later. There was much to do. The sacrifices needed to be presented to his deity. On the floor by his foot was Clarence's cell phone. He reached down and picked it up, hatching a plan. He smiled, knowing soon the world would see his dedication to Saint D'Inana!

And it will be a glorious thing!

Patrick set the phone up and looked at the curious device. And though he'd never used a cell phone before, Saint D'Inana filled him with the knowledge he needed to operate the phone, syphoning the power and required memories of those he sacrificed this day. He tapped the screen, then set it down so its camera provided a full view of the bodies, and pressed 'call' ...

•

The patrol cars turned the bend off the highway into the private drive leading to the Dark premises. Looking out the windows of the sheriff's cruiser, Dr. Pennoire noticed something odd near the first bend they came to in the drive. A section of the tree line was bent wrong. It was the width of a motor vehicle.

"Stop!" the doctor commanded, shouting her order with authority. Her driver relayed the message to his peers behind the wheels of the other cars. The order was carried out in precision, and the cruisers stopped in unison. Pennoire wasted little time in exiting her car. The flashing lights pierced the shade of the forest canopy. She entered the tree line. About twenty yards down the side of the hill sat a white van.

"This isn't good." She pointed down to the wreck; it wasn't visible from the road. The doctor's bodyguards flanked her to the left and right, their heads constantly moving, watching for any threat. A pair of deputies made their way down the hillside, slipping and sliding, banging into trees on the way. It took a few minutes to reach the van. Pennoire watched with anticipation.

"Nobody's down here!" one of the deputies shouted up.

"What's the plate number?" a sheriff on the road asked.

"X-Ray Bravo Bravo dasher niner niner Charlie Zebra. New York plate."

"Gotcha!" The other deputy read the numbers back to verify them. The deputy by the van gave a thumbs up in return.

"Over here, Phil!" the other deputy piped up.

"You find someone, Bernie?"

"Not exactly."

"What is it, Deputy?" Dr. Pennoire interjected, curious to know the result.

"A lot of blood, doc. A whole lot of fucking blood."

●

Ronnie Dark found himself in the backyard again. The shed and pump house sat before him; the late morning sun hung high in the sky, burning a spotlight down onto the lawn.

Ron didn't know what to do now. The cars up front were useless. He couldn't get away using any of them. His 'Vette was out of gas, and he doubted Balloon Boy would give him time to syphon from the tanks on Brodie's Jeep and the sheriff's patrol car. Ronnie was stuck here, trapped in his own mansion. He supposed he could take his chances, run down the driveway to the road and find some help. The only obstacle? A motherfucking killing machine nicknamed with affection by the media thirty-five years before as The Balloon Boy.

The boy was now a man with at least five more bodies to his credit. Lord knows how many other poor souls died on his trip from the looney bin up north. Without any other means, there was no getting away without going through said motherfucker. The guitarist knew he needed a weapon, and after losing the Mosin, the great equalizer in this battle, he'd take anything to even the odds against the game show quoting freak. He searched through the shed, tossing useless implements to the side.

He banged his infected finger on a tape measure. The adrenaline was wearing off, and Ronnie was reminded how much the hangnail sucked.

"What in the fuck?" he screamed. He tried shaking the pain off his hand. It didn't work. A roll of duct tape hung on the wall. He tore off a piece and covered the hangnail. It stung at first, but it wasn't exposed to air anymore, and this made a world of difference. Provided he didn't bang it around too much. Ron went back to the task at hand.

Find a weapon.

Except for a few long screwdrivers, there was nothing he felt could sway things in his favor. He pocketed the screwdrivers and pipe wrench. Frustrated, Ron grabbed a tarp off the floor and slammed the shed door closed behind him. He stomped over to the pumphouse and flung the door open.

The trio of dead bodies stared back at him, reminding him of the Hear No Evil, See No

Evil, Speak No Evil monkeys. He wasn't sure what bothered him more about them. Ronnie resolved it was less him seeing them and more of them watching him. He threw a nylon sheet over the three bodies. He made the sign of the cross with his hand.

A twinkle of metal next to Brodie's corpse caught his attention. It was a scrub slasher; the cutting tool was stuck into the wall.

That'll do, he thought in elation.

Ronnie grabbed the curved blade by the handle. The worn wood was sticky and black with the consistency of cold molasses and smelled like rotten meat. Ron could only imagine what combination of blood and guts it took to saturate the handle. He didn't care. He now possessed a weapon.

He could fight back.

Ronnie never felt so alive as he did at this moment, fighting for his life.

•

Patrick finished preparing his offering to Saint D'Inana, placing them on the bodies of the sacrifices. A dog from the guts of the man, representing his loyalty to his Dark Goddess; and from the woman, a crimson flamingo to compliment the Dark Saint's eternal beauty.

The sword vibrated with energy in his hand. He felt it course through his own body, giving him strength. And wisdom. Now he understood why the time would be now. He saw the lights and heard the cars shooting up the driveway to the house.

Patrick Dermotty slipped the Sword of D'Inana into its sheath and fell back into the shadows to watch and wait. It was easy for him to do. After all, he'd waited thirty-five years for today, to be reunited with his love.

Saint D'Inana.

Patrick stepped into the shadows falling from the mansion and forest canopy. They wouldn't find him, Saint D'Inana promised him, assured him. This was the perfect spot. He blended in with the darkness ...

Watching...

Waiting...

•

A sheriff's deputy jogged to Dr. Pennoire. She stared at him with cold, green eyes. The man was uneasy.

"The plates belong to a luggage return company in Brooklyn. We checked with the company, and one of their drivers, Mason Pilot, a twenty-three-year-old male, is missing as of last night."

"That makes at least three bodies, maybe four we're going to find. Wonderful. All because the New York State police couldn't be bothered to check the CSX lines running out of Fulton."

"We're ready when you are, Doctor." He replied.

"Let's go."

And they left. It was a few moments before Pennoire realized something was amiss.

The lights of the cars were flashing.

What the fuck are they thinking? She pulled out her phone.

"You had to go and announce our arrival like we're a fucking circus coming to town? Jesus, Mary, and the Saints. Are you amateurs?" Pennoire was on her phone with the deputy in charge, screaming at him.

"It's our standard rescue procedure, Doctor." he admitted; his voice sounded small.

"The whole point of sirens is to get the civilians out of the way, not to alert a mass murderer to our imminent arrival." Not wanting to hear any more excuses, she stabbed the phone, her fingernails cracking the screen, and ended the call. The lights went out on all three cars moments before they came to a stop at the foot of the small parking lot.

A red Jeep, belonging to the missing Steve Brodie. She was sure of it. *Our lost deputy's cruiser too.* Pennoire assessed the situation. A mountain of luggage stood on the porch to the house.

Alongside two dead bodies, each clasping something gruesome and bloody in their hands.

One of the deputies vomited off the side of the porch after he got a closeup view of the Balloon Boy's handiwork. Pennoire shook her head in disgust. These men were unprepared for this spectacle of evil.

"I don't like this, Doctor." Cunningham,

her pimply-faced bodyguard said. The stoic man spoke on rare occasions.

"Nor I," Rainwater agreed. Pennoire's ears perked and she raised an eyebrow. Rainwater was less conversational than her companion. "This is wrong."

"What is it?" Pennoire inquired. "What doesn't feel right?"

"He's somewhere near. Call it a hunch," Rainwater added.

"I'm of the same opinion," Cunningham corroborated.

"Interesting," Pennoire replied. She rubbed her hands together. "And where might he be?"

The doctor didn't have to wait long for the answer. Something caught her attention at the edge of the property.

"Patrick?" Doctor Pennoire asked.

•

Ronnie saw the cops and the lady in the long black coat milling around the driveway. He also saw the Balloon Boy standing at the edge of the property, clear as day, through the slits in the mask. They didn't know they were in danger. Ronnie knew it was his responsibility to warn them.

He ran from the backyard alongside the tree line.

Ronnie flailed the slasher in his hand, running as fast as he could to the deputies, trying to get their attention.

He succeeded.

A half dozen deputies all pointed their guns at Ronnie as if they choreographed the event. He saw this and damn near pissed his pants. He held his bladder, another minor victory in the shitstorm he experienced over the weekend, as he shuffled to a stop on the lawn. He threw his hands forward, dropping the slasher.

Behind the cops, Patrick stood in the trees, the sword in his hands, glowing and pulsing in the shadows.

"Don't shoot!" He screamed, "Behind you! He's behind you!" He pointed his hands. "Look!"

•

Patrick stood still and silent, watching the police officers aim their weapons. He saw Ronnie Dark too, still wearing his mask, allowing the guitarist to see Patrick in return.

Saint D'Inana, why do you test me so? he thought. The sword vibrated against his back.

To prove your worth, it seemed to say.

But haven't I already proven myself worthy? The sacrifices I've made for you. The blood and the souls you desired.

Saint D'Inana is a fickle mistress. She need not answer her servants.

They answer her.

•

"On the ground! Now!" one of the deputies commanded. Patrick watched as Ronnie said something they couldn't make out. A warning shot created an explosion of turf near his foot. The masked man fell to the ground and the deputies swarmed around him, their weapons pointed at him.

The doctor and her guards followed with

haste. Pennoire didn't waste a moment of time. She snatched the mask off Ronnie's head.

"It's Dick, he's alive!" She addressed the deputies.

"Dark, Ronnie Dark, not Dick," he protested.

The doctor ignored him.

"Where's Dermotty?" Rainwater asked.

"Good question, Brenda," Pennoire replied.

"I'm Ronnie! This is my house. The killer was behind you guys, up by the porch."

"What?" Pennoire pursed her lips and looked up at the house and the porch. She saw nothing but the luggage and bodies. "You guys see anything?" Bill Cunningham and Brenda Rainwater both shook their heads. "Great." Frustration fell across Pennoire's face. "Call in the choppers and get the FBI down here, stat!"

•

He watched as they spread out in his direction. Staying here would result in capture or worse: he would expose his Dark Goddess to the world. The world wasn't ready for Her. Patrick knew now was the time to go.

So did the sword.

Patrick closed his eyes and prayed in silence to his Dark Queen. He felt a disconnect from the now; he was weightless. And drifting away. He closed his eyes. His mind was swimming. His thoughts found themselves falling back to the time of the Saints ...

Patrick's mind spiraled and tumbled away. The mansion drifted away with his other senses. First obscured by the foliage, then by the mountain itself. The sword carried Patrick away from discovery by his pursuers.

Patrick fell deeper into the wood line. He felt the power of Saint D'Inana draw him away from the property. He felt the trees, the plants, the dead and living leaves, the former scattered across the ground, the latter clinging to the young growth. He moved through the forest, down the hillside and away from the mansion, retracing his path there, and away from here all together.

The motorcycle laid in the ditch where Patrick left it days ago, undiscovered. Saint D'Inana saw to it. Up the hill, he could hear the commotion, as the deputies searched the woods for him. He put Jamey's helmet and leather jacket on, kicked the bike to life, and rode away, down Route 42.

•

"It's not him! Put your guns away!" Doctor Pennoire commanded the sheriff's deputies. She helped Ronnie Dark up. "Doctor Amanda Pennoire. Please accept my apology. The mask. It was his."

"Yeah, I know, the mask. But he was right over there, I swear to fucking God." Ronnie pointed to the porch. "You let him get away."

"We didn't see anybody there. Do you really think he can get far? We're in the heart of the Catskills right now." Pennoire pointed at the porch, the deputies converged on the luggage pile and bodies near it.

"After what I've seen the last twenty-four hours, doc, I don't know what to believe anymore ..." And Ronnie Dark told Doctor Pennoire everything he went through in the last week as the Ulster County sheriff's deputies combed the property for any trace of Patrick Dermotty, the Balloon Boy.

Ronnie knew they wouldn't find him. Oh, they were about to discover a whole ton of dead bodies and carnage. But a gut feeling they weren't going to catch the Balloon Boy surfaced. Not today, at least. And he didn't give a shit. For the first time in a week, Ronnie Dark felt alive. Aside from the white-hot ring of pain throbbing on his left index finger, he was in pretty good shape, considering all he experienced. His duplicitous wife and her lover were dead. It was a bittersweet ending to their marriage, for sure. But Ronnie still breathed, his blood still pumped through his body, and nobody had made a fucking balloon anything out of his guts.

He felt a bit of remorse, a slight lamenting for Melissa, and even for Beaver. No one deserved to die in the manner they did. The same with Brodie and the others. He was going to miss Steve the most. The man was his oldest friend. Ronnie could afford a moment to mourn him, at the least. This brought a tear and he sniffled. He quickly regained his composure, though, fearful depression would take him back over. That was unacceptable. He didn't have a reason to die anymore.

Instead, Ronnie was seeing the potential to have millions of reasons to live. The publicity behind this could be his ticket back to the limelight. There was a story here, a big one, a story asking to be exploited. Ronnie could see it now, a movie poster in the drive-in screen of his mind. Ronnie Dark versus the Balloon Boy Killer! Books, a TV show. Maybe a reality series like Ozzy's, or a dating show, looking for a new Mrs. Dark, with a host dressed as the fucking Balloon Boy himself.

He would need to make a new list, this one featuring the people to call in favors from. The right publicist would be required, a new agent, one with aspirations for something other than a traveling tribute show. He could open the house to tours, like those demonologists the Warrens did with their place, except Ronnie's was the real deal, and the Warrens were full of shit. Merchandising plus marketing here would equal money.

Yeah. Ronnie Dark, formerly Ronald Dick, Jr., was standing in front of endless opportunities. The pain in his finger was subsiding, to the point where it was only a slight irritant. This was a good day, the start of something new and fresh for Ronnie fucking Dark.

All the excitement on a warm summer day parched the guitarist's throat. He looked at Doctor Pennoire and smiled.

"Anybody want some Kool-Aid?"

CHAPTER 24

BOB & PATRICK

SUNDAY, JUNE 13, 2021, 5:27 P.M.

The chime of an incoming ride request sounded across the speakers of Bob Foley's Kia Soul, drowning out the scream of Manowar's Eric Adams. He tapped his phone, watching the alert pulsate on his phone's screen. Bob was at first hesitant to accept the ride from *Staff Member*.

"Real cute name, buddy," he muttered. Then seeing it was a long ride, Bob got his hopes up for a really good pay day. So, he accepted the request.

•

Patrick Dermotty stood on the roadside, his sword from Saint D'Inana cleverly hidden behind his back, a hoodie covering his face. He held a cellphone and watched the phone's screen, ignoring the flying bugs of twilight swarming about it, crusted and dried blood caking his hands and fingers.

A bell rang on the phone, changing the color of the screen, and he smiled. Patrick looked down the road and saw a pair of headlights racing toward him. Red brake lights came on, and the car slowed until it stopped in front of him. It was a boxy, blue colored import with five doors. Patrick opened the back door and got in.

"Staff Member?" the car's driver asked.

"Will the real Staff Member please stand up!" Patrick said, holding the brim of the hoodie over his face and eyes. He climbed into the back seat of the imported vehicle.

"You're a funny guy. I like you already. Five stars, man! I'm Bob, I'll be driving you to Oyster Bay in Long Island, I see. Better buckle in, it's gonna be a couple hours to get where we're headed."

"Is there a letter Z?" Patrick asked.

"Hah! You're going to nap. That's fine. You got it, buddy. Any music you might want to hear?"

"What is The Dark?"

"You got it man!" The driver was animated in his response. The music played, Ronnie

Dark's guitar underneath Steve Brodie's vocals. Beaver's drums and Lightning's bass.

"Drink the Kool Aid!" resonated from the speakers and throughout the interior of the car. Patrick Dermotty buckled into the back seat, and Bob the Uber driver carried them away from the Catskill mountains of New York.

•

SUNDAY, JUNE 13, 2021 10:56 P.M.

When Bob Foley got home after his Uber shift and the long ride to Long Island, he was too wired to sleep. This activity was typical, he'd need some time to wind down. He'd been listening to good music all night, and it had his blood pumping. The last rider was quiet for the time he was in the car, and Bob could crank the music.

Looking at his phone, he saw it was just after eleven o'clock, and time for the late night news. Bob stripped down to his boxers, poured himself a glass of chocolate milk, grabbed a couple

Oreos, and sat down in his recliner. A moment later he clicked on the TV with a remote, and selected the local ABC affiliate's channel.

And his jaw dropped.

A live news report from Long Island graced his screen, and the setting is more than familiar to Bob.

He was just there!

"What in the ever-loving fuck?" He said as he watched. The lights of rescue vehicles flashed, and a news reporter stood in the center of the screen, delivering her lines.

"It's been a night of terror that started upstate in Fenton, spread down to Kingston, and ended here in Oyster Bay. We are at the home of renowned music producer Sandy Pearlman who was found dead in his residence late this evening. He's evidently the last victim of escaped serial killer Patrick Dermotty. Known as 'The Balloon Boy,' Dermotty was allegedly freed from Fenton State Hospital two days ago by his nurse, Kathleen Elizabeth White. White was indicated as the first victim in a chain of murders over the last few days, the majority of which occurred in Kingston, New York at the residence of musician Ronnie Dark. It is not known at this time how many victims succumbed to Dermotty's attacks, but the only survivor, Mr. Dark, is currently under Kingston police protection. The identified deceased include Ulster County Sheriff's deputy Jolene Stevens, as well as Mr. Dark's wife, Melissa Dark, and former members from his band, The Dark: drummer Clarence "Beaver" Allan and vocalist Steve "Brodie" Brudzinski."

The camera showed a middle-age man being led out of the house in handcuffs. Following behind him was an important looking woman, dressed in a long coat.

"Holy fucking shit!" Bob said, spitting out a mouthful of chocolate milk and chewed up Oreo pieces. The man in custody was his rider from earlier.

"Dermotty surrendered to authorities after making a call to 911, revealing his location. Dermotty allegedly murdered the home's resident, legendary music producer Sandy Pearlman, before surrendering to authorities. Pearlman produced and wrote the lyrics to many of the songs off the first six Blue Oyster Cult albums. Pearlman was also the producer of Black Sabbath's monumental album The Mob Rules, as well as The Dark's debut album, Don't Be Afraid

Of, which launched Ronnie Dark and his band into superstardom. Dark then used this money to purchase the home in which young Patrick Dermotty infamously murdered his family and friends during a sleepover, over forty years ago. This seems to be the only connection between the three."

"When questioned about his motive, Dermotty was heard to say 'He did it all for his love.' This 'love' happens to be a death goddess named 'St. D'Inana,' according to Dr. Pennoire, Dermotty's caring psychiatrist from Fenton State Hospital." The screen focuses on the dark haired woman in the long coat.

"Patrick's delusions make him think he's the avatar of a death goddess from a lost mythology, well, actually it's one he made up in his mind." She said to the camera, pointing to her temple as she elaborated on her patient's condition. "We're still investigating how Ms. White helped him escape from our facility. We'd know more, but as you already know, she was his first victim after his escape. I'm just glad we were able to recapture him before anyone else was harmed."

The camera returned to the reporter.

"Patrick Dermotty is currently in transit to his cell at Fenton State Hospital, with Dr. Pennoire. Authorities believe Dermotty was brought to the Oyster Bay by a ride share company, and they are currently awaiting confirmation on the whereabouts and safety of the driver. That's all we have for now. As more information is released, you can be sure to get it right here on your News Channel. Now back to you in the studio, Jim!"

Bob switched off the television and sat in silence, shaking. He Thanked the gods of metal for watching over him. *All Hail Ronnie James Dio, Randy Rhodes, and Dimebag!* He thought, knowing the bullet—or knife, more appropriately—he'd dodged on that night. He was tired, and could barely keep his eyes open. But right then, at that moment? He didn't know if he could ever drive rideshare, let alone fall asleep, ever again.

Then his phone's ring tone came to life, the opening drums and riff to Manowar's Blow Your Speakers resonated through his apartment. It played through multiple times before Bob grew the gumption to answer. The caller ID said

UNKNOWN CALLER but Bob Foley knew who it had to be…

•

MONDAY, JUNE 14, 2021 6:32 P.M.

Standing in his cell, Patrick Dermotty stared at the television showing an old game show, Press Your Luck. He may have appeared to be watching TV, but in his head, he held council with his love...

St. D'Inana hovered before him, shimmering through the dreamscape between the physical world and the otherside.

"I found the black mirror and opened the portal." Patrick said.

"Good." His goddess said.

"I read the words of the Azure Ones and have hidden the artifacts." He assured her.

"Good." She extended an incorporeal hand and caressed his shoulder.

"I now wait." Patrick said with pride, pleased his goddess was satisfied with his quest.

"Yes. Wait and celebrate." She told him.

"Celebrate?" He asked.

"With dance." She directed.

"With dance?"

"Yes. Honor me with dance." St. D'Inana *faded from Patrick's view...*

The programing on the television cut to a commercial. Chubby Checker appeared on screen, twisting the night away in an advertisement for a classic rock-n-roll collection. Patrick put one leg forward, pressed a toe to the floor, emulated Checker's movements on the screen... and danced.

Patrick Dermotty, the infamous Balloon Boy, who waited decades before to honor his dark goddess twisted his hips to the music and smiled as he prepared to wait again. He knew this time the wait would be shorter.

Much shorter...

THE END?

ACKNOWLEDGMENTS

The concept behind *The Death List* has long lingered within my brain, and it came to life about six years ago during a trip to New York City's Comic-Con. I recall telling my pal and journalism/podcasting peer Eric Cohen about it as we walked through the subways of Manhattan, when the working title was *Epic Fail*. But this book wouldn't exist without the assistance of Garrett Cook and Lisa Vasquez. They helped push me through the darkest parts of this piece, bringing it to a conclusion we all found satisfying. This is the toughest, and longest, piece I've brought to completion in my short career.

Though *The Death List* is set in the

Catskills and Ulster County, as a book, it is chock full of people I know from my regional area, much like my previous work *Bella's Boys*. To call much of this a nod to the Syracuse music scene would be an understatement. The book is littered with homages to musicians in central New York. Huge special thanks to Ronnie Dark for letting me use his name and allowing me to make Ronnie into what he always wished he could be, an 80s guitar hero. Jamey Arney, you're in here. Also, a shout out to Patrick Dermody, the Balloon Man who gives us all so much joy with his creations, and who inspired our slasher killer. And, of course, we can't forget my dear friends Steve Kratz and Tim Brudzinski, the inspirations for Steve Brodie, lead singer of The Dark. Mason Pilot—my trans godson, I made you a biological dude like you've always felt you should be. Jolene Stevens, a close family friend, and the first girl I ever thought was a girlfriend, who grew up to become an excellent State Trooper. Beaver Allan, the drummer in my oldest band, Cartune (and Lightning, the bassist!), and last, and certainly not least, Metal Bob "Foley."

For the record, there are also complete fabrications of people created for the narrative, including Melissa Dark. Of course she is a made up person. I wouldn't associate with someone as duplicitous as she.

At its core, *The Death List* is a parable about suicide. Suicide is a fucker. To some, taking your own life is a selfish act of cowardice. I can understand how a person would feel this way, but I tend to think not. I perceive it as an unfortunate result of an illness. I've lost two close and dear friends to this affliction in my life:

1 - Byron Brothers, my first "fan" as a musician. Twenty years ago, a week before Christmas he went to the spot he first made love to his estranged wife, and didn't come back. We congregated for his funeral the following week.

2 - William J. Barrett, my best friend. He and I were gaming foes, playing Magic, RISK, Titan, Axis & Allies, Hero Clix. You name it, we were Rommell vs. Montgomery, Montcalm vs. Monroe, Cromwell vs. Washington. We confided in one another, used each other to literally hide the bodies. I always looked up to

Bill, I saw him as a successful attorney with a big house and a perfect life. But it wasn't perfect. He and his first wife split up, and I was there for him through all of it. In more recent years, life and careers interfered with our time together. And just before the start of the pandemic, he and I started gaming together again. Then the pandemic hit, and he took his life. I'm still numb writing this today.

Be there for your friends and your family in times of depression. Be there for them when they push you away and when they run off. Remind them...suicide is pointless.

It's easy to tell a friend not to kill themselves. It's harder to prevent it. That's why professional counselors are available at your fingertips.

National Suicide Prevention Lifeline
1-800-273-8255

Thomas R Clark - 11/25/20

ABOUT THE AUTHOR

Thomas R Clark is a musician, writer, and podcast producer & engineer. He is the author of the 2021 Splatterpunk Award Nominated BELLA'S BOYS, GOOD BOY, and THE DEATH LIST—published through Stitched Smile Publications, and THE GOD PROVIDES, from St. Rooster Books. His journalism has appeared in Memento Mori Ink, Rue Morgue, This Is Infamous, and House of Stitched Magazine. Tom lives in Central New York with his wife and their canine companions.

THOMAS R CLARK